A ROSE MCLAREN MYSTERY

# MURDER IN MIDWINTER

# LIZA MILES

# MAD CAT
## PUBLISHING

Copyright © Liza Miles 2022

# Dedication

They say it takes a village to raise a child, and the fourth Rose McLaren Mystery could not have been completed without the support of my daughters Hanaa and Safia. The cats, Kate and Cleo, were completely hopeless word wise, but gave me lots of cuddles.

# Acknowledgements

With grateful thanks to Philip and Janet who pre-read the manuscript; to Annie for her endless patience combing the pages for grammaticals and to my editor and cover designer, Mary Turner Thomson.

# Chapter One

Rose fetched a tray from the kitchen and began to stack the remaining dirty plates and glasses from the tables on the patio; agreeing to cater a hen party for twelve demanding and entitled women two days before Christmas had ruined her plans to spend the holiday with Kay. One of the tables still groaned with the desserts, fruit, and cheese platters, following the sit-down dinner. Several champagne flutes were half full and there were shot glasses scattered everywhere she turned. She now regretted letting Trixie and Rob leave early, with the London guests. What had she been thinking?

It was after three in the morning by the time the patio was mostly cleared of its debris. Rose checked her phone, wondering if she'd missed hearing it ping with a message from Kay, to confirm she'd landed safely in New York. But it seemed Kay was still ghosting her. Rose didn't blame her, changing holiday plans at the last minute was not exactly the best start to the relationship Kay wanted for them both.

Rose lit one of the heaters and flopped onto a chair on the patio. Wrinkling her remaining good eye she looked out at the garden. Fairy lights were still twinkling on the shrubbery and inside the summerhouse at the bottom of the garden, in front of the rear wall. The bottle of Sancerre in the wine cooler she'd left deliberately on the table beckoned, the pale amber liquid untouched by the guests. Rose pulled the cooler closer and closed her eyes. Conflicted by the longing, urging her to take just one sip. A fake temptress deceiving her into believing she could stop. Rose tipped her head back and put the bottle to her lips. The light breeze intensified, outdoor decorations jangled like chandlery as the Christmas baubles clinked together, fairy lights danced and the wind chimes tinkled, tied bunches of dried flowers scattered across the lawn. Rose squinted as she watched the wind lift a pale blue satin kimono from the deck next to the hot tub. The fabric turned and twisted in its wind driven journey to the patio. Completing its dance, the delicate garment whooshed across the decking and settled against her foot. Thankful for the distraction, Rose put the untouched bottle back into the cooler. She bent down and picked up the kimono, she liked the sensation of the soft expensive fabric which smelled of perfume. Rose didn't recognise the scent and she didn't remember seeing anyone wearing the kimono earlier when some of the guests changed for the hot tub.

'Hello, is anyone there?' she called out into the darkness. Flicking the torch on her phone she waved it in the direction of the hot tub. But it was too dark for her to see, even if both her eyes had been working as they once used to.

'Hello,' she called out again. She heard a crunch as if someone had stepped on some glass. Rose stood up and waved her torch into the pitch darkness of the garden.

2

'Who is it? Are you hurt,' she called, then swung around quickly as the footsteps grew louder and she sensed the presence of someone close behind her.

Two arms grabbed her roughly by the shoulders. Rose brought her leg up behind her and kicked, her foot made contact with a sturdy, firm upper leg. She felt the fingers holding her arms loosen their grasp, she spun around, adjusted her balance. She tried to grab the face mask from the darkly clothed hooded figure but lost her footing. Rose collapsed down onto the floor of the tiled patio; she heard the wine cooler crash as it too hit the floor. Rose made a grab for it, but she was too late, she felt the blow to the back of her head before she lost consciousness.

By the time she came round, her attacker had gone. She looked around, to reassure herself that she was now alone and put her hand up to feel the back of her head. There wasn't any blood but there was a bump, the size of an egg, which was already protruding. She clambered up slowly, staggering slightly, she made her way towards the back door and turned the handle, but the door was locked. She knew she had locked the front of the house after Trixie and Rob had left and none of the windows on the ground level were open. She looked for her phone, feeling for it on the floor in the dark she cut her hand on the shattered glass from the wine bottle.

Whoever had attacked her must have stomped on the device, the screen was smashed and it wouldn't turn on. She felt sick and dizzy, she needed to get back into the house and started weakly banging on the door and then the windows. There was no response. She started to yell and bang harder but her attempts to rouse one of the

3

guests was useless. There was no sound or light from within the house. No-one came to her rescue.

Rose pulled on her reserves. She had to work out what to do and despite the patio heater, and the winter fleece, she was starting to get very cold.

She remembered there were blankets in the summerhouse and it also had an electric fire. That would have to do until the guests woke up. Breakfast was going to have to wait until Trixie arrived with the baking.

Rose made her way to the summerhouse at the bottom of the garden, via the decking where the hot tub was situated.. The cover was still off the top of the tub, the water would be cool by now. At least she could wash her hand which was oozing blood from the cut. Splashing her face in water would help her focus. It was as she drew closer to the decking; she saw the figure of a woman lying on the floor. Rose opened her mouth to call out, but the sound stuck in her throat; with horror she'd recognised the still and naked body was Belinda Sanderson, the bride-to-be.

Rose moved swiftly towards the supine figure and knelt down; the bride's eyes were open and bulging. She knew it was too late for CPR. A satin tie had been pulled tightly around the woman's neck – Rose subconsciously concluded it must be from the kimono that she had found earlier. One thing was certain, there wouldn't be a wedding now.

Rose ran back up the garden and roared, 'Help' at the top of her voice. Banging on the door again was useless. She lifted up one of the patio chairs and began to swing it against the door. Moments later the kitchen light flashed on.

'What on earth ...'

Wearing a bright pink onesie pyjama, Amanda, the bride's sister, arrived on the other side of the door and unlocked it.

'Where's your phone?' Rose demanded 'Or the landline. Quickly!'

Amanda pointed at the wall opposite the island. 'Why were you outside with the door locked? You're bleeding!' Amanda grabbed a tea towel and flung it at Rose.

'Someone attacked me, but ... look you'd better sit down. There's no way to say this nicely. Belinda's dead and I need to call the police.'

Amanda wailed, staggered backwards onto a couch near the phone and stared blankly, while Rose called 999.

# Chapter Two

When Trixie arrived at Torphichen Street with the breakfast baking at 7am on Christmas Eve, the house was taped off and closed. Rose had left a message on Trixie's mobile telling her not to come.

Trixie, not recognising the unknown number, explained to the police that she hadn't had time to listen to the message. 'Ah've brought the breakfast, can ah nay just bring it in?' But the police wouldn't let her, or anyone, in or out.

DCI Hickson hadn't seemed surprised to see Rose at the house. The two women had met before. Dubbed the ice queen, DCI Hickson and Rose had warmed to each other when Rose's dogged pursuit for information had led to charges and an arrest in a previous murder case.

The bride's body had been photographed then moved to the morgue for further examination by the time the DCI was ready to interview Rose and find out exactly what she had seen and heard. The police had turned the elegantly furnished drawing room at the front of the house into a temporary interview room. Another junior officer, a man called Jones joined them.

'So Rose, do murders follow you around or is it the other way around?' DCI Hickson put her head on one side while she waited for Rose to answer.

Rose shook her head. 'Honestly, I'm beginning to wonder. It wasn't what I expected to happen when I opened up Muffins on Morrison.'

DCI Hickson raised one eyebrow. 'It's not your usual gig, is it, living in and catering? How well did you know the deceased?'

'I didn't. I know her sister Amanda, she's a regular customer. She owns the barre and yoga studio a few doors up from the shop. I only met Belinda yesterday afternoon. She was … She was so alive, full of excitement about getting married. Amanda had organised everything. It was a last-minute booking and she was desperate. It meant I had to change my plans too. I should have been in New York with… With a friend.'

'When did you accept the booking?'

'Two weeks ago. Amanda had originally booked everything with another local company who specialises in catering for this type of thing. I don't know what happened, but Amanda was desperate. I had to say yes. I've re-booked my flight to New York for the 26th.'

'We may need to ask you to stay in Edinburgh. I'm sorry.'

'It's okay, I may not have gone anyway.'

After a few more questions about timing - who, when and where Rose had last seen particular guests and what she had done when she found the body - DCI Hickson drummed her pen against her leg. She appeared to be contemplating what to ask Rose next and leaned forward. Then, apparently changing her mind, she looked at her colleague and spoke to the junior officer. 'Jones, can you get some tea organised?'

Hickson waited until the man left before she said, 'Rose, I know from meeting you before, you have good instincts. Did you hear or see *anything* that suggested Belinda's life was in danger?'

'Honestly, no. The afternoon and evening were full of the usual hen party shenanigans. Too much wine, too much giggling and to be frank, I was trying to avoid being part of anything that wasn't to do with the food. Hen parties are really not my scene. And the group were, shall we say, demanding. Except for the bride actually. She was very sweet. Amanda tried to manage the others, but the ones from London were a pretty entitled bunch.'

'How many guests were there?'

'There were seven  staying here and another five who came for the evening, they arrived about four in the afternoon.. The guests who weren't staying all left in a taxi together. There was a bit of a fuss because the taxis had come early. Anyway shortly after that I sent Rob and Trixie away. I was staying overnight in the downstairs suite off the kitchen. I was about to lock the back door when I realised the outside patio still needed cleaning up.'

'Rose, once you leave here, can you go over everything again? Anything at all that you heard or saw, maybe making one of your maps will jog your memory. And if you don't mind, if you do remember anything please let me know directly. Don't leave a message.'

Rose nodded, surprised and pleased the woman had remembered how she figured things out. 'Yes of course.'

'Sorry we had to send Trixie away with all that baking. A muffin would be very welcome right now.'

'Yeah, agreed. I'll bet Trixie is fuming. She'd have been in the shop from 4am getting it all ready.'

'Thanks, Jones,' the DCI said, as the man came back with a tray of tea.

'Shall I continue with the notes ma'am?'

'Yes, please do.'

The DCI brushed back her blonde hair from her face and tucked it behind her ears before she resumed her more formal style of questioning.

Rose left the house on Torphichen Street just before eleven. Amanda, the dead bride's sister, had tried to persuade her to stay so they could talk, but DCI Hickson had made it clear she was not in favour of any discussions between them until she had finished questioning everyone.

'Call me on this number Rose if you do think of anything however small or insignificant it seems. Call anytime. I'll not be taking any break over Christmas now.'

'Sure,' Rose said and pocketed the card.

Without a working phone, Rose couldn't let Trixie or Rob know she was on her way to the shop. It was Christmas Eve and their regular customers had all been notified the shop would close at midday. Most of the customers would just be picking up orders, they weren't expecting too much in the way of passing trade. The vegan Christmas cakes she and Trixie had designed had proved really popular. Once her customers had taste-tested them and posted reviews online the cakes had been in demand and flying off the shelves since mid-November. She'd also created a spiced almond orange cake mix for gluten-free customers in an elegant, gift-wrapped glass jar. All the gift recipients needed to add was juice from an orange and a lemon and four eggs.

Trixie was sweeping the floor when Rose arrived. Not one morsel of baking was left on the shelves or in the window.

'Rob, Rose is back,' she yelled. She scurried out from behind the counter and threw both her arms around Rose. 'Are ye arit? Ah was so worried.'

Extracting herself from the bear hug, Rose nodded. ''Yes, I am but I need a big strong brew and something to eat. One of the muffins from the hen party breakfast if we still have them. Have all the orders been picked up?'

'Aye, that wis the last leavin' when ye arrived. Oh my god Rose, wha' happened?'

'The DCI wants to talk to you, to both of you,' Rose inclined her head to greet Rob as he emerged from the kitchen. 'Until then, she's asked me not to talk about what happened. In case our conversation muddies the waters about what you might have seen or heard.'

'Really?'

'It's her way of doing things I suppose.'

'Sounds stupid to me, and she's always been frosty'

Rose held up her hand, 'Actually she's not quite the Ice Queen we'd all painted her when we first met. This morning she even remembered how I made maps to figure things out on that last case.'

Rob whistled. 'I can see where this is going.'

'Well, maybe. She's asked me to see if I could remember anything, so I might create a map, see if I think of anything I might have missed. But first I need to replace my phone. Look.' She took the damaged device out of her pocket to show them.

'I'll come with you; I need to buy a few bits. We're all done here aren't we?' Rob looked around, the shop was clean and tidy apart from Rose's mug and a plate of crumbs.

'Yer no' still tae buy gifts Rob, surely.' Trixie leaned over and gave Rob a playful punch.

'Ian's difficult to please.'

'Ay rit. Yer full o' nonsense.'

Rose rolled her eyes mocking the banter. 'Ok, you two, let's go. I'll come back and finish up anything else that needs to be done. I'll drop the wedding party baking over to the shelter, unless you want to take it to yours, Trixie. Aren't you having company?'

'Ah am but nae, everythin's already bought. Rob, wit aboot ye?'

'I'm alright, Ian's mum has bought enough for the whole of Glasgow.'

'Aw, for her wee boy and his lover! Guid luck wi' yer phone Rose an getting to yon big apple.'

'I might not be able to go now, not with the police investigation. And anyway, Kay still hasn't ...'

'Oh Rose, in that case, come to Glasgow. I'm sure Ian and his mum won't mind. I'm not leaving you by yourself.'

Rose put her hands up. 'Thanks Rob, but I'll be OK. I'm seeing Anthony tonight and honestly, resting up will do me good. It was mad thinking I could go to New York and get the new shop ready for opening by February the first, as well as hiring someone for here, now that Trixie has finally agreed to take on managing the new shop.'

Trixie and Rob looked at each other and grinned.

# Chapter Three

The restaurant was packed with family groups and couples when Rose arrived to meet Anthony Chatterton. He stood up and waved at her from the corner window table he'd reserved specially. 'Happy Christmas. I'm glad you could still make it for dinner with me after the day you've had. How is your head now?'

'I'm fine, there's a pretty big bump though.'

'And your hand? What happened?' Anthony nodded in the direction of the finger dressing.

'Whoever attacked me stomped on my phone, I cut my hand on a broken wine bottle trying to find it. Oh let's not talk about it. I've had enough of death and murderers to last me a lifetime.'

The server attended to their order and set them up with water, a complimentary cocktail for him and a mocktail for her.

Then Anthony leaned in and spoke softly. 'There's something I wanted to talk to you about. Although, if you've had enough of talking about death, I don't know if I should.' His hand gestured towards a large brown envelope on the table next to him underneath a small gift wrapped box.

'OK, this sounds serious for Christmas Eve. I may be done with murder but I'm not done talking about you. Are you alright? Is everything ok with your heart?'

He smiled, then patted the left side of his chest. 'I'm really fine and I'm much healthier than when I was a policeman.' Anthony pulled his phone out of his jacket pocket and using his fingers enlarged a photograph. It was of the dead girl . Belinda Sanderson. She was in the middle of a group of people with her arms around her fiancé. 'When Trixie texted me earlier to tell me what had happened and that you didn't have a working phone, I was watching the news. They were covering the story but hadn't given out the girl's name or any details. Then later, they published this picture of her with her family. I knew there was something familiar about her face but I couldn't place it. Anyway I went back through some of the files I'd kept, unfinished business and I found this.' He reached into the envelope and pulled out another group photograph with a young girl of about ten holding the hand of an older man. 'Look at her face, and then the picture of Belinda Sanderson, the woman you found murdered.'

Rose sat back in her chair, her face drained of colour as she stared at the photograph of the child holding hands with Olifer Hoffman, the man who'd killed her friend Chris and gotten away with it. Rose studied both images closely. 'God, do you *really* think this child is … is Belinda? I mean children's faces change.' She screwed up her good eye and studied the pictures again. 'It could be her, but the police are still looking for Olifer. Do you think he would risk coming back to Edinburgh, for her wedding I mean?'

'If he does, he would be in disguise, and definitely not as Oliver Moorcroft this time, He is the master of hiding in plain sight.'

Rose shook her head. The game of murder that Olifer Hoffman had played the last time he was in Edinburgh rankled. Whoever had allowed him to get away with murder had a lot of power. Anthony had been diligent following up information, however minute, and passing it on to the authorities, but the fraudster and killer remained a free man. 'We should tell DCI Hickson about the connection.'

Anthony smile, 'How are you two getting on?'

'Alright actually she asked me to reflect on what I saw yesterday, make a map.'

'Hmm, you melted her frozen heart, did you, and made a good impression.'

'Apparently.'

'How come you took that job, catering for the hen party? Why didn't you fly out to New York with Kay?'

'I don't know to be honest. When Kay suggested New York for Christmas and New Year I was so excited. But then, and I haven't told anybody else this, I got scared. What if it all went wrong? When Amanda begged me to cater the hen party, it was a way out. I could make an excuse without telling Kay that I was having second thoughts about everything.'

Anthony sighed. 'I know how that feels, Rose. To want to be with someone and then not want to be with them because you might screw it up. But you and Kay seemed happy together, after you'd finally decided to move from friendship to dating.'

'And now I've pushed her away. I don't think she's talking to me. Even if I wanted to go out to New York on the 26th I don't think I'll be able to.'

'How?'

'The investigation.'

'The police can't ask you not to travel, so long as they know how to get hold of you. You're a key witness, not a suspect.'

Rose pursed her lips and then excused herself to go to the bathroom. Weaving her way through the closely packed tables of diners she reflected on what Anthony had just shown her. Finding Belinda's body had been bad enough, now there was a connection between the murdered girl and the man who had murdered her last lover. But Rose also knew something deeper, and more troubling, was at the root of the conflict she was experiencing. She fixed up her face and made her way back to the table.

'Trouble is, I know I don't want to go to New York. I've been lying to myself. And now you've shown me this, the connection between Belinda's family and whatever it is with Olifer, I definitely can't go. I need to put Chris first, it was my fault he was murdered.'

'Rose, listen to me. The only person who is to blame for murdering Chris is Olifer. Don't let him ruin your future. He will be brought to justice. I promise you that.'

'Do you think Amanda knew about my connection to Olifer, that I was his half-brother's lover?'

'I don't think you should pursue it. As you said we should tell DCI Hickson about the connection and then let her do her job.'

'Louise,' said Rose absently, staring at the plate of food, which was almost cold.

'What?'

'DCI Hickson, she told me her name, it's Louise.'

'That sounds pretty chummy. Look, why don't you join me and some friends tomorrow, it's a house party for single waifs and strays.'

'Thanks, but I'll be fine. I don't really *do* Christmas, you know that.'

'OK, but then no arguing. I'm paying for your taxi home and let's order you a slap up meal from here to take home so you don't have to cook or make do with leftovers tomorrow.'

Rose ran a scalding hot bath and changed into clean pyjamas. Then she poured out the contents of the envelope Anthony had given her. As well as the photograph of Belinda and her fiancé, Anthony had printed out a copy of Belinda's family tree, but there was no mention of any connection to the Hoffman family recorded there. Then Rose spotted it. According to the copy of her mother and father's marriage certificate in Switzerland, their nuptials were witnessed by Olifer and Sylvia Hoffman. Rose stared at the paperwork. Had Amanda really had an ulterior motive when she asked Rose to cater the hen party for her sister?

# Chapter Four

Despite it being Christmas Day, thanks to the murder, DCI Hickson was spending the remainder of the day at the police station. That morning the Torphichen house had been searched again and cleared for the London guests to move into. She took her time studying the photograph Rose had brought in, along with the picture she had printed out of Belinda with her fiancé. Looking through a magnifying lens the DCI studied the other people in the older photograph. It was faded and not very sharp. 'Where did Anthony get this?'

'I don't know, Switzerland maybe. He did a lot of digging and travelled to Europe to build up the file. He didn't think the photograph was useful because, at the time, he didn't know who any of these people were.'

'It's odd Belinda is in the picture, but I can't see Amanda, or the parents. She's about eight or nine I would think. Thanks for bringing this down Rose, I don't know how useful it is in regard to Belinda's murder, but he,' she tapped the top of her pen against the photograph, 'is still a wanted man and not just for murder. I don't like unresolved crime. I'm sorry, I understand one of his victims was a close friend of yours.'

'Chris, yes. Hoffman is, or was, Chris's half-brother.'

'I'll do what I can. Did you have any thoughts about what you saw or heard before Belinda died? Did you see or hear anything that struck you as odd?'

Rose shook her head, then took a sip of the watery tea that Jones had brought into the interview room. She looked around her and thought about how many times she had sat in that same room since opening her shop. The cream walls, the single light bulb and the wooden desk with four chairs hadn't changed over the five years. The only difference was who was sitting opposite her and how open they were to what she had to say. When he was a DCI, Anthony Chatterton hadn't welcomed the information she'd offered him initially, but she had grown on him and now they were good friends. After her own dad died they had become very close, and Rose often confided in him.

'Anthony has been quite determined to find Hoffman and get justice for Chris. Finding this connection between the dead girl and Hoffman will have stirred him up again.'

'Rose, try to talk him down will you?. Last thing I need are two amateur detectives getting in the way.'

'Oh, believe me, I'm done with sleuthing. Seeing Belinda like that, I'm not going to be getting involved.'

DCI Hickson raised her eyebrows and was about to speak when Jones tapped on the door again. 'Sorry ma'am, this is urgent.'

Rose stood up and offered the DCI her hand. 'Good luck with getting to the bottom of it all. I'll continue to think and let you know if I remember anything that could be helpful.'

'Good to know. Thanks again.'

A light flurry of snow started to fall while Rose made her way home on her e-bike to Corstorphine from the police station. She looked up at the sky, it didn't look like it would last long, she could risk staying out a little longer. She turned around and headed towards her shop on Morrison Street. If she went home she wouldn't be able to settle and the shop would benefit from a really deep clean. There would be no danger of interruptions today she thought as she cranked up her music and set to, scrubbing, and washing everything to within an inch of its life.

Rose had almost finished in the kitchen, the low haunting pipe at the beginning of Dire Straits' *Telegraph Road* was playing when she heard someone banging on the glass door of the shop. Rose sighed and went to see who it was.

Amanda Sanderson burst through the door, her face was red and puffy from crying. She was wrapped in a thick blanket and wore the same onesie she'd had on the night before, when Rose had found Belinda's body. She looked as if she had neither slept nor showered for the past twenty-four hours. 'I can't believe what you've told the police. How dare you suggest our family has anything to do with that horrible man or Belinda's death. You're a monster. I'm going to post your disgusting business all over social media, ruin you. You ...' Amanda took a breath, her body deflated like a burst balloon as she collapsed sobbing onto the chair by the window table.'

Rose closed the door quietly and stood back to let the woman recover herself. Her sobs were raw emotion, grating, painful to listen to. Rose knew that pain all too well. The anguish of feeling betrayed, volcanically erupting before subsiding into a pool of sadness.

'Would you like some water?' Rose said as the sobs became softer with gentler gasps for breath.

Amanda nodded. 'Please.'

Rose poured two glasses of fresh water and sat opposite Amanda. 'I'm sorry if what the police told you made you think I blamed you. I couldn't keep the connection hidden once I knew about it. Your uncle murdered a good friend of mine.'

'Olifer Hoffman *is* my uncle, but I have nothing to do with him.. Something happened between him and my parents before they died, an argument, then he stole my mother's inheritance. We never saw or talked about them again. Good God Rose, I would never have asked you to help cater the hen party and breakfast if I thought anything would happen to Belinda.'

'We don't know how or even if the two things are connected. The person who pushed me over and knocked me unconscious certainly wasn't your uncle. Wrong build, wrong height. I don't know if it was a man or a woman. And why on earth would your uncle kill a niece he hand't seen for years? Unless there was money – was there?'

'Yes, but not any that he could get his hands on. That's what I told that policewoman, she's a cold fish.'

Rose smiled, 'Yes I used to think that too. But actually she's very good at her job. Trust her, I'm sure she will find out who is responsible for Belinda's death.'

'Will you help, Rose? I know that you've been involved in helping solve other crimes, you single-handedly rid the street of that monster who was making drugs on Morrison Street, when you first opened up your shop.'

'Don't let the police hear you say that. I'm sorry Amanda, my amateur sleuthing days are over. I've put my friends in danger in the past, and now I only have sight in one eye, with the other failing fast, I can't risk it again.'

'I didn't realise about your eyes, I mean, you're so competent, confident.'

'I'm good at wearing a mask. I'll do everything I can to help the police. I keep going over everything in my mind about what I saw and heard when I was catering for your guests. Who were they all by the way, not family?'

'No, and I'm sorry, the women from London weren't very nice, but I didn't really know them. They know Belinda from her work as a publicist for a publishing house. Very entitled.'

'Very,' Rose agreed. 'Are they all still in Edinburgh?'

'Yes, we rented the house until after the wedding for a few days. The group from London were supposed to be moving in today. The police told me they'd finished doing what they needed to do. But I haven't been able to get hold of any of the guests. The police want everybody to stay in Edinburgh, but perhaps they've changed their minds about using the house now.'

'Can you think of anyone who'd want to hurt your sister?'

'No, she's such a … was, such a sweet girl. Even when we were growing up we rarely fought. Although, I was sent to boarding school, so we kind of didn't really grow up together.'

'The picture I gave to the police, with your uncle and Belinda in a family group. Where were you and your parents?'

'I think that must have been the day I was taken off to school. Belinda was eight and I was eleven. There'd been a family party and we had all gone to Germany. That's where I went to school.'

'In Germany, why?'

Amanda shrugged. 'My father thought an international school was going to be better for my future. He was an academic, a modernist. He believed in unity and a world without borders.'

'But Belinda didn't go there?'

'No. She went to school in Edinburgh, then for A levels, they sent her off to London. Which was odd because I'd come back to study here in Scotland.'

'So really you two didn't spend much time together once you turned eleven? Yet you seemed very close.'

'We were. We used to write when we were younger and then when Skype and Facetime were invented we talked pretty much every day. She was my best friend, not just my sister.'

'And her fiancé? When did they meet?'

'Leo works in publishing, they met at a book launch. It was a bit of a whirlwind romance. I don't really know him to be honest. She told me about him maybe six months ago, then in September she announced they were engaged and wanted a Christmas Eve wedding in Edinburgh. Kilts, bagpipes, hand tying, white heather, a ceilidh, the whole shebang.'

'Is Leo Scottish?'

'No, his family were from Kent, but they moved out to America when he was a child.'

'Ah, hence one of the guests at the hen party being American?'

'Yeah, Leo's sister - Caroline. Another charmer, not!'

'She was a little difficult, I did notice.'

'I'm sorry about earlier, I just needed to … I don't know what I needed to do, but after the police left I was really shaken up. I guess I needed to blame someone.'

'It's OK, I get it. Been there. Got the T-shirt for unbelievable behaviour. Look, what I said earlier, about not being able to really help, why don't you give me the list of guests, their names and anything you know about them. I'm not promising anything and I have promised DCI Hickson I won't interfere, but sometimes I see patterns when I make maps. I used to be a pilot.'

Amanda looked up at the photographs on the wall of the shop. 'You look great in the uniform. Why did you leave, was it your eyes?'

'Yeah, that and a very bad man!'

'There's a lot of them about Rose. OK, I'll email you the guest list I gave to the police. Thanks.'

Rose finished cleaning up the shop and thought about what she had learned about the relationship between the two sisters. She wondered why the parents had separated the girls when they were growing up?

With the take home dinner Anthony Chatterton had ordered for her heated up, Rose studied the list of names Amanda had emailed to her. Apart from the twelve women from the hen party there were twenty six other guests. Rose tapped her pen against her leg. Thirty eight guests was a small wedding given the type of celebration Amanda had described Belinda wanting. Perhaps because neither the bride or groom had parents who were still alive they had concentrated on people who knew them well, rather than extended family members such as cousins or aunts and uncles. She opened up a copy of the family tree Anthony had given her and compared the names, but none of Belinda's relatives appeared on the guest list. The bride hadn't invited any family and, apart from Caroline

Monkton. Leo hadn't either, unless they had different family names, which was possible.

She closed her eyes and tried to remember what she had seen and heard before all the guests went up to their rooms in the house on Torphichen Street. Belinda and Amanda were sharing the ensuite master bedroom on the second floor, Caroline had her own room on the first floor along with Mhairi. The other three women were at the top of the house. Rose put a question mark on the paper and drew a diagram of the bedrooms where each of the women had slept. She did the same with the dining room and named where the guests had been sitting, as far as she could remember, then she repeated the exercise when the guests were in the garden, in the hot tub and on the patio. She couldn't remember the timing of where everyone was exactly, but she was beginning to remember noticing how Belinda engaged differently with the guests from London and that Caroline had been very reserved, kept to herself, for most of the evening. Rose remembered she had overheard Kyla being annoyed about the top floor bathroom, but that was later after everyone had gone to bed.

Rose wrote down the order and the times she remembered things happening. The women staying in the house had arrived just after three. They chatted and ate afternoon tea in the dining room. They went upstairs to change while Rose tidied up. Trixie and Rob arrived and helped serve the canapes just before the London guests arrived, just after four pm. After that everything seemed to run smoothly, dinner was served at seven thirty, desserts and cheeses went out just after nine.. The women had played games inside and then went out into the garden for a hot tub, which is when Amanda had asked Rose to move the platters of food onto the patio. Everyone came back inside around midnight and they played more games. Then the taxis arrived. Caroline had already gone upstairs. Rose, Trixie, and Rob were still finishing off the dining room and kitchen when the house guests, including Belinda, went upstairs. Trixie and Rob left just after the London guests. After that she had set the dining table ready for the morning, then realised the patio needed clearing.

There was no way she wouldn't have seen or heard Belinda come downstairs and go out into the garden. The front door was locked and she was certain no one had entered the house through the front or back doors after Trixie and Rob left. Either Belinda hadn't gone upstairs with the others or she had somehow slipped past Rose without her seeing. And, if she hadn't gone upstairs, where were her clothes, the pale green sparkly top and black leggings she'd been wearing all evening? They hadn't been on the deck by the hot tub or on the patio.

Her phone pinged with an email from the airline, reminding her to check into her flight to New York, scheduled to depart at ten the next morning. There was still no message from Kay. Rose sighed and cancelled her booking. Then messaged Kay to let her know she wasn't coming. She could see Kay was active on WhatsApp and waited for a reply. Even being told she was a bad friend would be better than silence.

No message came.

# Chapter Five

The flurry of snow from yesterday had turned into a blizzard overnight. The pavements outside Rose's flat were sparkling as the morning sun caught the deep virgin layers of snow. The bright crisp morning tempted her out.

After a breakfast of porridge with blueberries and strong coffee, she found herself walking towards the house on Torphichen Street. There was no sign of a police presence and the curtains and blinds were all closed. Rose rang the bell, but there was no reply. She fumbled in her pocket; she still had the key Amanda had given her. Glancing up and down the street Rose unlocked the door and closed it quietly behind her.

'Hello, is anyone home?' She waited in the hallway at the bottom of the stairs, then made her way through to the kitchen. There were several bowls and dishes in the sink and a number of cups and glasses on the island. It looked as if the hen party had cleared out after the interviews on Christmas Eve and the London women had decided not to move in once the police had opened the house up. Rose washed up the plates and glasses and then went upstairs to the master bedroom Amanda had shared with Belinda. Belinda's wedding dress was hanging up outside the wardrobe along with an open suitcase full of what looked like honeymoon clothes, mostly beachwear, strappy sandals, underwear, and sundresses. There was no sign of the outfit Amanda had worn during the hen party.

Rose opened the wardrobe, but it was empty. Then she looked in the dresser drawers and checked the bedside tables. She was about to leave the room when she noticed a book on the chaise longue at the bottom of the bed. It was a proof copy, marked *not for sale*. Some of the pages had been torn out and were lying loose next to it. It wasn't just a romantic read, Rose realised; the torn pages described an explicit sex scene and some of the writing was underlined.. She took the book down to the kitchen and placed it in a plastic freezer bag.

She had just opened the door to go out into the garden when she heard a floorboard creak upstairs. She paused, waiting to see if anyone would come down. Whoever was there had been very still and silent up to now, which meant whoever was hiding was hiding from her. She didn't want to play a prolonged game of cat and mouse and decided to call out to them.

'Hello, it's Rose the caterer, I'm in the kitchen, who's there?' She went back to the kitchen to get her phone to call the police when she heard footsteps running down the stairs and the front door open. The light coming through the front door created a shadow and Rose stumbled as she ran from the kitchen into the hallway, by the time she arrived at the front door she only caught a brief glimpse of a woman in a dark green tracksuit, her hair covered with a baseball cap, getting into a silver car; the car sped away before Rose had the chance to take a picture or get the number plate.

She went back inside and ran upstairs; she tried not to touch anything in case she contaminated any evidence from whoever had just fled from the house. The door to the bathroom opposite the master suite was open, she was sure it had been closed before. She looked around and saw the access panel under the side of the bath had been pulled open. Using the torch from her phone she peered inside, reached in, and brushed her hands across the floor. Whatever had been there was gone. She trod carefully and went into each of the other bedrooms, trying to find the creaking board. The flooring looked new and nothing in the other rooms had been disturbed, although given the unmade beds, it was hard to tell if someone *had* slept there overnight. The spare guest room that no one had used was immaculate.

She went back downstairs into the back garden. There was still police tape around the hot tub but the summerhouse door was wide open. Rose looked inside. Blankets were strewn over the L shaped sofa, the mirror on the back wall was askew, several plants were on the floor with soil spilling out of the pots and the rattan coffee table was on its side. A fragment of what looked like a business card, pale grey speckled cardstock with part of a logo was lying next to it. Rose picked it up carefully at the edge, just in case it contained a fingerprint.

She was torn about whether to call Amanda or DCI Hickson first. The intruder was long gone. The woman who'd run out of the house could have been anyone with a slim build under five foot five, which described most of the women at the hen party except for Caroline. Not even a wisp of hair had been left outside the cap and Rose's eyes were not sharp enough to describe the profile of the driver.

She'd presumed it was a man driving but she couldn't be certain.

Rose decided to call Amanda first. 'Can you get over to the house?'

'It had to be one of the London women you saw, apart from you they are the only other people to have a key,' said Amanda, handing back the plastic bag containing the fragment of card and the book to Rose. 'I don't recognise that logo though. Belinda often read steamy romance type books as part of her job; she enjoyed them. But I don't remember seeing her reading the night we were at the house. You say the book was on the chaise?'

'Yes, did you read this?' Rose pointed to one of the paragraphs on the torn page. 'It describes a sex scene where the woman is being partially choked by a satin tie from her dressing gown.'

'No, that's horrible. I don't think Belinda was … wait, are you saying you think Belinda's death was rough sex gone wrong?'

Rose shrugged. 'With who? The DCI will know if she'd been sexually active before she died, but outdoor sex on a freezing cold night would be risky with me clattering about the place, cleaning up in the dining room and the kitchen. The rooms both overlook the garden. Then of course the patio was still a mess and I was out there clearing up for quite a while before I found her. Could Belinda have let Leo in without anyone seeing?'

'No, he was at his stag do until very late. I know that because my friend saw him and sent me a photograph. The group were being pretty rude to a server in one of the late night bars, one of Leo's mates had grabbed her and put his hand down her blouse. And, well between you and me, from what Belinda said, he wasn't into anything kinky.'

'Charming, I hope the server slapped him. Look I need to tell the DCI about the intruder and this book, I just wanted you to know first, in case what the police told you sounded like I was making out Belinda was, well you know.'

'Yeah, thanks Rose. Appreciate it. There's something else, I've not been able to get hold of Mhairi, the other bridesmaid since Christmas Eve..

'Oh, did you two leave together?'

'No. She was the last of us to talk to the DCI. She had asked to wait until we were all finished. By that time I'd already left the house. I called her that night to see how she was and go over what had happened. I called her again, before I stormed over to yours on Christmas Day. She's not responding to my texts and she isn't showing as active on any social media sites. Usually she posts something every day, and she loves Christmas. Although of course, after what's happened to Belinda, she's probably too upset to do Christmas posts this year."

'Did you call her family? Could she be with them?'

'I called her mum, they're in the Highlands and her fiancé is away. He wasn't going to make it to the wedding. His family were having a bit of a do, down in Wales, the timing sucked. Mhairi was furious when he told her he'd chosen to go to Wales. Even so he was expecting to speak to her, they'd arranged a time on Christmas Day, but she didn't answer him either. Nobody has heard from her.'

'Sounds a little odd but maybe she's just hiding away until she feels lie talking to someone. I do that. Being alone, it's not always the best answer though. Do you know anything about the author of the book? Do you think Belinda knew her?'

'No idea, she probably did, through work. It's the same publisher Belinda did publicity for.'

Rose pulled her laptop closer and typed in the name of the publisher and author of the book. Whoever the author, Bea Lion was, there were no images. The publisher had listed the book as scheduled for release the following year. Rose tried a different search engine, there were still no images for Bea Lion and no social media accounts for a writer with that name.

'Well that's odd, I guess it is a pen name. Maybe a writer who doesn't want to be associated with writing steamy sex, apart from picking up the royalties.'

'I wish you had some idea about who's been in the house.'

'Sorry, she flew down the stairs and was out of the front door into the car like a bullet. I do know the car wasn't there when I arrived. Either I disturbed her and she called someone, or she let herself into the house after I went in. The door wasn't locked at that point, but I'm sure I would have heard someone come in. I think she took whatever was stashed under the bath, she was carrying a bag of some sort. I think it was green, but as you know my eyes aren't all that... I mean maybe that has nothing to do with Belinda's death, although it doesn't seem likely. Look, I really should call the DCI. Do you want to be there when I talk to her? You could talk to her about  Mhairi as well.'

DCI Hickson's demeanour was cool and guarded when she arrived at Torphichen Street. There was no acknowledgement that she had in anyway invited Rose to offer her thoughts or insights when Rose gave her the package with the book and fragment of business card.

The DCI shook her head. 'Where did you find this? Why didn't you call me straight away, we've lost over an an hour because you delayed. Unfortunately this is a blind spot for CCTV, so we won't be able to identify who came in, the car or the driver. You said it was a man driving. Are you sure about that? Couldn't it have been a woman?'

'I don't know exactly, but the size, shape, although look at me I'm five eight, so it could have been a taller, bigger woman. The woman who got in the car was definitely smaller, slim, fit. About your height.'

'But you couldn't identify her. Are you sure?' DCI Hickson studied Rose for a moment then turned to look at Amanda. 'Who was using the bathroom where the panel was moved?'

'It would have been Mhairi and Caroline.'

DCI Hickson nodded, 'Could Mhairi have been the woman Rose saw?'

'No, no, Mhairi is so straight and honest, she wouldn't even have a clue how to tell a lie, let alone have anything to hide under baths. She's also quite well built. She was my friend as well as Belinda's, we've known each other for years, since we were children. Mhairi is in the middle of us, age wise, she was like our other sister.'

'OK,' DCI Hickson said, 'but that doesn't mean she's not part of this somehow.'

'Well you were the last person to have seen her. Was she really upset after the interview? No one has seen or heard from her since she left here.'

Hickson stiffened. She was about to reply when one of the officers tapped on the door and came in. 'Ma'am, you'd better come and look.'

'Wait here you two. I'll be back.'

'I know Mhairi couldn't have had anything to do with Belinda's death, or this morning, whatever that cold hearted woman says.'

Rose reached out and drew Amanda in for a hug. 'She's just doing her job. Look, are you sure Mhairi hasn't gone up to her parents or to Wales since you called them?'

'Absolutely, we've kept in touch. And now with the news of the murder all over the news, they're extremely worried about something might have happened to her too.'

Rose checked her phone. Amanda was right, news of the murder had made all the major papers and television news. The headlines were salacious and brutal. *Christmas Bride-to-Be Strangled* and *Lovers Knot Kills Naked Bride Before Vows.* 'Looks like the press are gunning for Leo, look at this headline and the copy.'

'Oh poor Leo. He had nothing to do with Belinda's murder.'

'It gets worse, look at this.' There was a photograph of Belinda on a beach in France in a yellow bikini. A woman was rubbing suntan lotion onto her back while a man was holding both ends of a long yellow silk scarf wound around Belinda's neck. They were all laughing. 'Have you seen this before?'

Amanda shook her head. 'No, but I recognise both of them from a party I went to in London,' she pointed at the man and the woman in the photograph, 'He's a photographer, she models, they were both invited to the wedding.'

When DCI Hickson returned she was holding an antique earring, a cream pearl set in the middle of blue sapphires. 'Do either of you recognise this? Jones found it in the summerhouse. I don't know how it was missed yesterday.'

'Yeah, I do, it belonged to our mother. Belinda was going to wear them for the wedding. She didn't have them on for the hen party, she was wearing silver hoops.'

Rose nodded. 'Yes, I remember that, definitely silver hoops, but she wasn't wearing any earrings when I found her. Did you find her clothes by the way? A sparkly top and leggings. I don't remember seeing her wearing the kimono or changing for the hot tub.'

'No. We did take some clothes from the bedroom that were on the chair. A red blouse and black skirt. We assumed that's what she was wearing before she changed into the robe.'

'I wished you'd asked me.' said Amanda, 'I would have told you that wasn't right. Those were my clothes. I wondered why you'd taken them.'

DCI Hickson made a face. 'That shouldn't have happened. I'm sorry. I'll speak to Jones and make sure you get them back. Can you come with me, back to the bedroom and see if the other earring is still there? We've already combed the garden and the summerhouse where we found this one.. Would she have loaned them to anyone for the hen party?'

'No, definitely not, they were too special.'

'Have you seen this?' Rose held her phone out to the DCI to show her the newspaper article with the salacious headlines.

'I don't believe it!' Her cheeks flushed as she read the copy and swore under her breath. 'You didn't hear me say that. I promise you Amanda, I will get to the bottom of it.'

'I don't understand. Do you mean someone has leaked information to the press, someone from the police?'

'I don't know who spoke to the press, but will find out and when I do, I promise you heads or a head will roll. The last thing we need is for the investigation to be compromised.'

'The last thing I want is for my sister to be laughed at or her reputation to be trashed, the way this makes her look and sound, it's horrible. Look at the comments people have left.'

'The paper will be wrapped around chips tomorrow, not that that's still allowed, but you should be more concerned about what's online. The internet doesn't stop. Try to stay off it and ignore the haters. I'll do everything I can to find out who killed your sister,' the DCI said as she bustled out of the room.

Amanda started to shake, her face bereft of colour she clutched at her chest, she was blinking fast and making small snorting noises as her body gasped for breath.

'Breathe,' commanded Rose, 'like this, look at me and breathe. It's just a panic attack. What brought that on?'

'Amanda followed Rose and began to breathe deeply.

'What brought that on?'

Amanda shrugged. 'I don't know, I get them from time to time, I mean, 'I ... '

'What is it?'

Amanda opened her mouth to speak, then closed it again. She looked at her phone and mumbled, 'It's nothing, don't mind me. I'm just a mess.'

Rose bit her lip, 'If you know anything, now would be the time to tell the DCI.'

# Chapter Six

'Aww Rose, the shop looks braw,' Trixie called out, taking in the gleaming interior, as she clattered through the door, laden with bags and a gift wrapped box.

'Thanks. But what are you doing here? We're closed until the 3rd January. This is supposed to be your holiday, before you never have time for one again!'

'Aye, ah know, but ah couldnae wait any longer tae give ye this. Ah hope ye like it.'

'Trixie, we'd agreed no presents.'

'Och, ye cannae gi' me a bonus and no' expect me to spend a bit.'

'On yourself! Oh, come here, thank you.' Rose stood up, put the box Trixie handed her on the counter and then hugged her. 'Tea?'

'Thanks, thought ye'd ne'er ask.' Trixie grinned. 'Ye look pretty guid Rose for someone who's nae where she's supposed tae be; an, who found the dead bride who's all o'er the news.'

'I'm ok. Did the DCI talk to you?'

'Ay, ah've nae heard from her since. Rob too. We went an signed the statements together on Christmas Eve, before Rob went to Glasgow. Yer still nae thinkin' aboot poking yer nose in?'

'I didn't poke my nose into anything, I just happen to ...' Rose stopped and laughed out loud, 'Honestly why do I put up with you?'

'Cos ah mak' ye laugh,' Trixie said with a chuckle.

'You do. I'm going to miss having you here with me, but I'm really really glad you'll be running things over at Queensferry. You're a safe pair of hands. This shop would not have become so successful without you being part of it.'

'Oh just open yer box Rose, ye'll hae me cryin' in a minute.'

Rose had just untied the ribbon when her phone rang. It was Amanda.

'Did you listen to the news? It's about Mhairi?'

'No, I've been cleaning and preparing our new recipes all morning, for when we open. Has Mhairi turned up?'

'No, well yes, her body has. Rose, she's dead! A fisherman found her at Loch Leven, she'd left a note in her car. She drowned herself on Christmas Day.'

Rose paused and took a deep breath. 'Are the police certain it was suicide?'

'Yes. Her mother called me about an hour ago, when the story went public.'

'Do you want me to come over?'

'Oh yes please, I need your help. I have to know what the police aren't saying. I mean, it has to have something to do with Beli doesn't it? Why would Mhairi kill herself?'

'I don't know, don't jump to conclusions, grief takes people in different ways. You said yourself you were like sisters.'

'Yes, so why didn't she talk to me? We were all upset, devastated, we should have helped each other, this is my fault, I shouldn't have agreed to … Please Rose, I don't know what to do.'

Rose closed her eyes and waited. What was Amanda afraid to tell her? 'You shouldn't have agreed to what?' Rose sensed Trixie staring at her, willing her to say no to what was being asked and not get involved in helping solve a murder.

'I'm scared Rose. If what we did comes out …'

'Ok. I don't know how much help I can be, but yes, I'll try. But Amanda, don't hide secrets, it doesn't help. I'm on my way to yours now.' Rose clicked off her phone and looked up. Trixie was shaking her head from side to side.

'Och, I cannae believe ye've promised tae help. Leave it up to the police.'

'I can't Trixie. Amanda's afraid of something, someone and she's keeping something from the police. I don't know whether I am getting involved because of what happened to Chris and the guilt I feel about what happened to him, now that there's a possible connection with Hoffman.'

Trixie's mouth flew open. Rose had forgotten that Trixie had no idea about the photograph Anthony Chatterton had found and the connection between Hoffman and Belinda's family. 'Let me fill you in quickly.'

'Ah think ah should come wi' ye,' said Trixie as Rose put on her coat.

'Really? Don't you have plans with …'

'He's away to see his gran for the day, so ah'm all yours.'


'Thanks for coming,' said Amanda as she let them in the door to her flat. The place was awash with unfinished cups of tea and partially eaten food on different plates sitting on the floor and coffee table. 'It's a midden here, but I couldn't face coming out to you.'

'Nay worries, ah'll get tha' all cleaned up and a fresh brew made.' Trixie said as Rose put her arms around Amanda.

While Trixie busied herself with clearing away the debris, Rose guided Amanda over to the squishy patterned couch and sat next to her. She pulled a throw from the back of the sofa and wrapped it around Amanda's shoulders. 'You've had a nasty shock, first Belinda and now Mhairi. But you need to take care of yourself. When did you last eat?'

'Beli's hen party I think. Every time I make some toast, or try to eat I just feel sick.'

'OK, well let's try and get some hot sweet tea into you while we talk.''

Amanda nodded and pointed to two letters on the coffee table. 'I think you should read those first. I haven't told the police about them yet, but I know I'll have to.'

The first letter was from a publishing company that Belinda had worked with as a publicist for different authors.

*Belinda,*

*It has come to my attention that extracts from a manuscript you were contracted to read for publicity purposes, have recently appeared on the internet, under a different title, accredited to a different author.*

*The leaked information has been identified by our IT department as coming from a laptop, owned by this company, registered on loan to you. This breach of confidentiality is a major violation of our working agreement and we have advised our lawyers accordingly.*

*You must immediately refrain from further use of the laptop and return the device to IT within the next forty eight hours. Failure to comply will result in criminal charges against you.*

*Sincerely*

The second letter was from the publishers' lawyers, reiterating the same request to return the laptop and an invitation to a meeting. Both letters were dated three months ago. The third letter was from a different publisher, WwW, offering Miss Bea Lion a publishing contract for her submitted book with an option for two further books featuring the same protagonist. The letter and contract were dated October last year.

'Hang on, I thought the book written by Bea Lion was with the same publisher Belinda worked for?'

Amanda nodded. 'I didn't know that Belinda used the name Bea Lion to write. I just thought she was doing publicity for the book. What I don't understand is, if she wrote the manuscript, why was she being accused of leaking it? And how could she have two publishing deals for the same book?'

'Did Leo, her fiancé know what she was writing?'

'I've no idea. But the company he works for publishes women's fiction, including erotica intended for the female market. You can ask him if you want. He's coming over to give me the gift he and Belinda had bought for me for organising the wedding. He called just after I spoke to you. Is that ok?'

'Yes, yes of course, I'd like to talk to him.'

Rose re-read the two letters and took a picture of them on her phone. Amanda was right she'd need to pass these to the police. Her instincts that the book was somehow important had been correct, and she wondered why the book hadn't been bagged in the first search.

'Is this what you were trying to keep quiet about?'

Amanda nodded.

'You sure, there's nothing else?'

Amanda pulled her shoulders up to her ears and moved further down the couch away from Rose. 'That's it,' she said.

'Ok. Remember the book that was on the chaise longue that I found, with the torn pages. You said you didn't see Belinda reading when you stayed there, but do you remember seeing the book at all?'

Amanda pursed her lips and tilted her head to one side. 'I don't think so, but there was so much going on, I had endless lists I kept checking, making sure I hadn't forgotten anything, I was pretty distracted. Even for a small number of guests, the event took a lot of organising.'

'Where did you find these letters? Was there anything else with them?'

'Beli brought a huge case of stuff with her when she came up from London, she said she wanted me to store it for her. You're welcome to look through it. These were tucked into one of the outside pockets. I rummaged through the inside of the case, but I didn't see any other paperwork.'

'Maybe she filed everything else electronically.'

'Well there was no device anywhere and I've no idea what happened to her phone.' The police combed the house looking for it, but they didn't find it. She rarely had it out of reach. '

'I'm still curious how she ended up outside after you had all gone upstairs. I didn't see or hear Belinda come back downstairs when I was clearing up the kitchen. The ground floor, apart from the front room and the hallway, is open plan. Would she have been wearing the kimono and her clothes? Theoretically she could have snuck downstairs into the front room without me seeing her, except she would have had to come through the kitchen to get out into the back garden. Amanda, are you OK?'

Amanda's eyes glazed over, she began fiddling with the ribbon on the neck of her pyjama top.

'Where was Mhairi when you went upstairs?'

'She went straight to her room, no wait, I heard her in the bathroom. Caroline had to go upstairs to the bathroom on the second floor because Mhairi was there for ages. I heard her come out and call goodnight while I was brushing my teeth in our ensuite. Beli was already in bed.'

'And the other guests?'

'Straight to the top floor. Sally, the hairdresser, and a make-up stylist from her salon were coming at 8 in the morning. The timing was already tight, fitting everyone in, if they weren't up early enough.

'And you weren't aware of Belinda leaving the bedroom once you were in bed?'

'No, she was already asleep. The light on her side of the bed was out.'

'Why did you share the bedroom? After all, there were enough spare bedrooms available.'

'We wanted to. We thought it might be the last time we would now that she was getting married.'

Rose had been taking notes while she talked to Amanda. She turned back a few of the pages in her notebook and looked at the first drawing she'd made, where the guests had been sitting and staying. She tapped her pen against the paper in a steady beat while she considered what Amanda had just told her. Something wasn't right, but she had no idea what it could be.

Trixie had finished tidying and came through from the kitchen carrying a tray loaded with mugs of tea. She had warmed a plate of the curried muffin samples Rose had baked earlier and which they had brought with them.

Amanda looked around the room and raised her eyebrows, 'I can't believe what a difference you've made in such a short time.'

Rose winked. 'She's a marvel isn't she. That's why she's getting her own shop to manage.'

'Och stop it. Ah'm nae paragon o' virtue as well Rose kens.'

'A new shop. Really? That's great news. Where?'

'South Queensferry, prime location for tourists and locals. We were lucky to get the space when it came up for rent.'

'Congratulations to you both. I'm sure it will be a great hit, just like Muffins on Morrison is.'

'Well try and get a few bites of this down with the tea,' said Rose, handing Amanda a mug and a plate. 'I'll go and have a look through that case.'

'OK, it's open on the floor of the spare bedroom, to the right of the front door.'

The case was full of framed pictures, two photo albums, cocktail glasses wrapped in bubble wrap, some china ornaments and three exotic skimpy costumes that wouldn't have looked out of place in a pole dancing club. Rose flipped through the pages of the photo albums. There were pictures of Belinda growing up, some with Amanda and Mhairi and a selection of tickets and programmes for concerts and theatre shows. Rose looked closely at the shots of Belinda when she was about the same age as she was in the photograph Anthony had given her, but none of these pictures included Olifer Hoffman. There were several framed photographs of the girl's dead parents, some with their daughters; and others unframed, with groups of friends at what looked like a wedding. Again Olifer Hoffman didn't feature in any of them.

Rose unwrapped a couple of the glasses and then some of the ornaments. The ornaments were the sort of thing a child might have bought as a holiday souvenir, except for one. A hand painted ceramic ginger jar. When Rose opened the lid she was surprised to find a USB stick taped to one side. Rose carefully removed the USB and put it in her pocket.

Amanda had been right about the paperwork; all the pockets and compartments were empty. She emptied the case of all the contents, patted on the lining, checked back inside the pockets and was about to put everything back inside when she realised the mechanics of the metal handles weren't working smoothly. She opened the access panel and saw a small, tarnished silver coloured key taped to the side, preventing it from being pulled up.

The style of the key was old. It looked like it would be used to open a cabinet or a desk drawer. Rose looked back through the photographs searching for a clue as to what or where the key belonged. But she found nothing useful.

She went back into the living room, Amanda was laying on the couch, covered with the throw. Her eyes were closed. It looked like she had managed a few bites of the muffin. Trixie put her finger to her lips and moved silently towards the kitchen. 'Find anything?'

'Possibly.' She held her hand open to show Trixie the USB stick and key. 'These were both well hidden, which is why Amanda didn't find them. I'd like to find out what's on the USB before Amanda shows it to the police.'

'That key though, it looks ancient, ye've nae hope in finding wha' it opens.'

'I'm not giving up yet!'

'That's me telt, aye, course ye will.'

Rose was about to retort when the bell to the flat rang. 'That must be Leo, Belinda's fiancé.' Rose went to wake Amanda, but she was already up from the couch.

Leo was tall, with a mop of curly brown hair, there were dark circles underneath his deep brown eyes. Rose offered him her hand. She was surprised by the thin, slippery grasp as their fingers met. His stature suggested strength and a regular workout. Rose assumed his professional position in the publishing world would usually assure anyone he met that he was competent, capable. Today he seemed incapable, as if the outer embodiment was a mask. Be fair Rose, she told herself, he has just lost the woman he was about to marry. She gave him a gentle smile. The usual pleasantries people uttered after a death didn't seem appropriate, so she said nothing.

Leo handed Amanda a gift wrapped box. 'I hope you'll like it, she … Beli … she went to a lot of trouble to find it.' His voice almost choked on the name.

'Thank you. Come in, have some tea. I think Rose would like to talk to you if that's alright.'

'I've just come from the police. I'm talked out right now. Sorry.'

'That's alright,' said Rose. 'Maybe later or tomorrow?'

45

'I'm going back to London later. That detective, have you met her before? She was trying to prevent me from going back to London, but apparently she can't stop me. God, it was like, like she thought I'd killed Belinda, after I told her what Mhairi had said. ' His face turned red as he spat the words out. 'I'm just bloody angry about how incompetent she is. It was you that found Belinda, is that right?' He pointed his finger towards Rose.

'Yes.'

'So how come the police don't suspect you, I mean, isn't it usually the person who finds the body? Oh no of course, not when it's a woman. It's always the boyfriend or the husband who is to blame with you women isn't it?' He was no longer weak or slippery, as he pulled himself up. The superior strength of his body was on full display, like the feathers of a strutting peacock.

Rose took a step back and put both her hands up, palms facing outwards towards Leo, 'You know none of us here think you had anything to do with Belinda's death. What you're feeling right now, all this anger, it's completely normal. Everyone is devastated by what's happened.' Her strategy worked, seconds later his puffy bravado had gone, Leo sank down and reached out for Amanda.

'I'm sorry,' he whispered.

Amanda led him through to the living room. She put her arms out and they fell into a hug on the sofa. 'None of us have heard from Mhairi, but you've talked to her?'

'Yeah, Christmas Eve, about four. She was heading out of town to a cottage. She said she needed some space.'

'Oh, Rose, sounds like you were right. What did she say that made the DCI so angry?'

Leo batted his hand in the air. 'It was dark, and she'd been drinking. She was just muddle headed I think. It didn't really make any sense.'

Rose fiddled with the USB stick and held it up, 'Amanda, can I use your computer to check this out? I found it in the suitcase.'

Amanda nodded and pointed to her laptop on the desk in front of the window. 'Password is SundaySunshine97, cap S on both words and no spaces.'

'I'm assuming you don't know what's on here. It might be better if I took your laptop into the kitchen, just in case what I find is ...'

'What do you mean?'

'The costumes in the case, could she have been working at something else?'

'She kept them?' Leo jerked his head and looked towards Rose.

'Maybe you'd better tell us about them, Leo.'

Leo put his head in his hands and moaned. 'I don't believe it. She promised me.'

'Leo, you're not making any sense. What did Beli promise you?' Amanda said, her voice shaking. 'I'd assumed the costumes had been something to do with her work for the publisher. Some of the covers she showed me in the past were pretty risqué.'

Leo bit his lip. 'One of the photographers talked her into doing some shots for him, for a cover. We had a huge fight when she told me about it. It would ruin her career as a publicist. She told me she wasn't going to do it and she'd return the costumes to the stylist. But ...'

'But what?'

'Oh something between us, I said she should have photographs done just for me. Maybe that's why she kept the costumes. Sorry, that makes me sound like a sleaze.'

Rose uploaded the USB into the computer and opened it. 'It looks like she lied about not doing the covers.'

'I don't think I want to see,' said Amanda.

Leo made his way over to the desk and leaned in, close to Rose. There were various shots of Belinda dressed in different costumes, including one with the yellow scarf, from the picture on the beach the newspaper had published. After the photographs, there was a series of different artwork for book covers, all featuring Belinda, with titles that would appeal to readers looking for fetish romance.

'So she's not Bea Lion here. Do you know who the author is, Leo?'

'No.'

'And the photographer, is he this guy?' Rose pulled up the newspaper article she'd saved on her phone.

'Maybe. The woman is his girlfriend, she often models for book covers and specialist magazines.'

'Erotica?'

Leo nodded.

You knew they were both coming to the wedding?'

'Yes, of course. He was at my stag party. She and Belinda were friends before we got together. That picture with the yellow scarf was taken in Barcelona. Some of the books, when they get translated, have different covers, using local locations. I remember Beli going on the trip. She sent me the photograph from there. But I don't know how it ended up in the paper, unless ...'

'Unless what?'

'He could have given it to them. He'd do pretty much anything for money. And what the police already think about Belinda and me is pretty disturbing. Once they find out about this, well they're not going to take her murder seriously, are they. For god's sake Belinda, why didn't you listen?'

'Oh shut up Leo,' Amanda spat across the room. 'Of course the police will take it seriously, all you seem concerned with is how you're seen. Well I don't care about that, I just want whoever killed Belinda to be found. Stop blaming her.'

'I'm sorry, I don't mean to; I loved Belinda. Please believe me.'

'I think you'd better go.'

Leo sighed and gathered up his jacket and bag. Rose followed him out into the hall and handed him her business card. 'I would like to talk to you - will you call me when you arrive back in London?'

'If you think it will help. Sure, and I'm sorry about what I just said and before. You're right, feeling angry is normal.'

'I know the feeling well,' said Rose as she closed the door.

# Chapter Seven

Mhairi's suicide and her connection to Belinda, who the papers had now cruelly dubbed *Dead Sex Romp Bride*, was all over the news the next morning. Rose had made a zipped file of the USB stick contents and Amanda had handed over the original to the police. Rose kept the key. Amanda agreed they would tell the police they found it later, giving Rose time to see if she could find what it opened and what Belinda had been hiding.

Rose cleared the wall behind her couch and fixed two large white poster boards on the wall. She transferred the original map she'd made about the Torphichen Street house, a photocopy of the picture of Belinda on the beach and a cover from one of the books on the USB stick onto one of the boards. On the other board she put a copy of the picture of Belinda as a child with Hoffman. DCI Hickson had suggested a map to stimulate her memories about the hen party, now the map was driving Rose's dogged determination to solve the murder and bring Hoffman to justice. Like a chess champion she saw patterns in moves that had already been made and moves that were possible. She knew she could work it out if she was savvy enough to focus on the seemingly unimportant details. When Rose was training to become a pilot, emergency manual aeronautical charting had been one of her strengths. She used the same skill to maintain her equilibrium in the bad times, after she'd been released from prison. The strategy to focus on the small things helped her strive for sobriety; it wasn't usually big life events that tempted her to escape reality.

Rose made a pot of coffee and stared at the boards. She thought about the bottle of Sancerre on the patio, how the flying kimono had interrupted her when it fell at her feet. And then she realised what had been bugging her since Amanda had told her Belinda was already asleep when she climbed into bed. This was a locked room mystery in reverse. Whoever had attacked her on the patio had locked themselves back inside the house. The main door couldn't have been opened and locked again from the outside because the top and bottom bolts were still in place when the police arrived. Unless her attacker had leapt over the wall of either of the neighbouring properties and then through the six gardens on either side to the main road or side street, they had to have gone back inside the house. But, the back door, and the door down to the basement were both locked from the inside.

Rose recalled each one of the guests from the hen party to mind. Amanda, Belinda, Mhairi and Caroline were easy enough but she was less clear about the three women in the upstairs rooms. She checked the booking slip and guest details about allergy or food preferences she had asked Amanda to complete. Kyla and Neive were based in Scotland. Sinead had flown over from Germany, where she was studying music. Recalling their faces, size and weight, none of them seemed likely assassins although Rose knew better than to rule anyone out. She had almost lost her own life by making that mistake. Strangulation with the dressing gown tie suggested a personal crime, something planned. The attack didn't look like it had been a frenzied spur of the moment impulse. The way Belinda's body was laid out, almost posed, could have been of a book cover, where the intimate parts of the model were blurred, or hidden under a bold macabre style typeface. She looked at the book covers from the USB, Belinda hadn't posed as a victim in any of them; if anything, she would be considered the dominant party.

The fact that Mhairi was dead didn't rule her out as a possible suspect. Rose also reluctantly included Amanda in her list. Caroline was the tallest and, apart from Mhairi, would have been the strongest of the guests. Like her brother, Leo, Caroline looked like she worked out regularly. Rose put a star against her name - she could easily have overpowered Belinda or even herself without too much effort.

Rose was about to start calling the numbers Amanda had given her when her buzzer went. It was Anthony Chatterton, bearing a take-away lunch of vegetable tempura, sushi and noodles.

'I called Trixie to find out where you were likely to be,' he confessed as Rose expressed happy surprise and let him in.

'You could have just asked me,' said Rose, clearing her dining table of papers and her laptop. 'How was your Christmas for waifs and strays?'

'It was very good. Surprisingly well organised. I err ...' He stopped himself and smiled. 'Are we just doing small talk now?'

Rose chuckled. 'Okay, there's a reason you're here and I'm glad you are.' She pointed to the wall with the poster boards. 'Look familiar?'

Anthony nodded. 'Oh yes, but I'm glad that this time you're doing this on your wall, rather than mine. Less danger of us falling out.'

'Indeed,' Rose said recalling the argument that nearly ended their friendship, after her pig-headedness had almost got her killed.

'Let's eat while the food is still warm and I'll fill you in,' he said, removing his jacket and taking a paper file from his bag.

.oOo.

'You seem to have friends in powerful places,' Rose replied after she had listened to what he had to tell her. 'How long has Hoffman been back in Edinburgh?'

'He comes and goes under the name of Lance Cooper, he owns a flat on the ground and middle floor in a conversion at the end of Dean Park Crescent, the property changed hands last year.'

'What the ...?'

'Exactly.'

Rose stared open mouthed at the amount of work Anthony had done since they last met. 'How come the police don't know about any of this?'

'Rose, remember who we are dealing with. I'm sure someone does. The same someone, or group of people, who helped him flee and prevented him from being arrested for murder and everything else he was involved in. I'm going to pass what I've found out to DCI Hickson. I can't keep it to myself, even though I'm guessing nothing will happen. I want to make sure Hoffman is eventually brought to justice and the more I hand in ...'

'Well let's hope someone does eventually take notice. I suspected Chris of being the murderer remember?'

'I know. The way you talk about him, Rose, even though it was a brief relationship, I think you loved him.'

Rose took a sip of water and looked down. 'Well I usually seem to make a mess of any close and personal relationships; look how I've treated Kay.'

'You still haven't heard from her?'

'Nope and I don't expect I ever will.'

'I'm sorry.'

'Me too. Thank you for showing me all this. I don't see how Hoffman could be connected to Belinda's murder though. Do you?'

'I don't think he is. It was remembering that photograph that gave me the nudge to see what else I could find out.'

'More like a shove than a nudge, from what you've put together here.'

'And you've decided to find out who murdered Belinda. What happened to you being done with sleuthing?'

'This feels personal. I mean finding her like that, and getting to know Amanda, her sister.'

Anthony put his hand out and patted hers. 'Please be careful.'

'I will. You too! If you're determined to continue finding out about Hoffman. I can't help with that while I'm trying to figure out who killed Belinda. Much as I would want to.'

Anthony changed his glasses and moved closer to the poster boards. 'What do you know about the women you've listed here?'

'Not a lot, I was about to try and contact them to meet up when you arrived. And I'm waiting for Leo, the fiancé, to call me. He left a message earlier, it was a bit cryptic, he said he was going to talk to the police in London, something about Mhairi, but I was in the shower. He's back in London.'

'Is Leo a suspect?'

'I don't think so, but the DCI gave him a grilling and he knows something, I'm sure of it. Even though he couldn't possibly have been there that night. He was photographed by a friend of Amanda's at a club that night, he looked pretty wasted. I'm thinking it has to be somebody staying in the house. You've heard that one of the others, Mhairi, committed suicide? Could you ...' Rose paused. 'The autopsy for Mhairi. I mean is it possible they could be saying it's suicide when it isn't?'

'Sometimes a murder can be made to look like a suicide, but the pathologist and crime scene investigators are pretty quick to spot it. There's usually an obvious mistake. So I doubt it. Why?'

'I guess I don't want her to have been the murderer. I don't know why, I hardly knew the woman.'

'Maybe you should just concentrate on getting your new shop up and running and leave this to the DCI after all.'

'That's what Trixie thinks too. Oh, did she tell you to say that?'

Anthony grinned. 'Maybe. But we both know that once you've made up your mind there's little anyone can say that will change it. I was also going to let you know, but that'll keep. I'll tell you another time.' he held up his hands and gave Rose a wave

.oOo.

Although she was curious about what Anthony was going to tell her, Rose turned her thoughts back to Amanda. She knew something about that night, so what wasn't he saying? She tried returning Leo's call, but it went straight to voicemail. She sent him a text with a photograph of the key, asking him to call her as soon as possible. Then she dialled Caroline.

'The caterer woman! Why are *you* calling me? Amanda shouldn't have given you my private number.'

'I'm sorry to disturb you. I'm trying to help Amanda, she's obviously in quite a state about what happened to Belinda. You can check that out with Amanda or your brother Leo if you want. Are you still in Edinburgh?'

'I'm here until tomorrow. That damn policewoman has been very unreasonable. But she has no choice. I'm going to stay with Leo in London for New Year. I've told the police everything I saw and heard after we all went to bed. That girl Mhairi was forever in the bathroom so I had to use upstairs. I exchanged words with Kyla after I used the facilities, then I took one of my pills and went straight to sleep.'

'Sleeping pills?'

'Natural stuff, they work when I'm away from home. I find it hard to sleep otherwise, especially on the sort of bed in that horrible little bedroom. I don't know why Belinda had to drag everyone to Scotland. What was the matter with a decent hotel in London? At least I could have had a proper shower.'

Rose bit her lip. Caroline wasn't the type of woman she warmed to. 'How well did you know Belinda? I understand the engagement happened soon after she met Leo.'

'Yeah. Honestly, I didn't know her at all, I came over for the wedding out of duty to Leo and because my folks were too busy, as usual. Belinda seemed OK, Leo's usual type, petite, blonde, blue eyed. She was less vacuous than his last girlfriend, she told me she was going to run her own publishing house one day. I didn't take it seriously.'

'How come?'

'You do know that our family founded one of the oldest and largest publishers in the world?'

'But Leo works for …'

'One of our imprints. It isn't doing as well as it should be, which is why he came to London.'

Rose made a note to ask Amanda what Belinda had said about Leo's role. What Caroline described seemed quite different.

'Does that mean Belinda was working for your family, on that last book she was reading?'

'I don't get involved with any of that, I'm focused on the bottom line. Profit. The way my daddy trained me. Leo's the one who likes to get his hands dirty on the front line.'

'Right. Well, thanks for talking to me, I'll let you go, you must have a lot to organise.'

'Not really,' and without another word she ended the call.

Rose pulled up the photographs of the letters to Belinda from the publisher, which she'd stored on her phone. Maypole was the imprint of Leo's family business, Monkton Press. They had two other imprints called Wildflower and Tanjay which specialised in sub-genre romantic and fantasy fiction. The publisher who had offered Belinda a contract was called WwW. The proof of the book Belinda had been reading was going to be published by Maypole. But, if Bea Lion was Belinda, why had Maypole threatened to take legal action against Belinda for her own work?

Rose looked up WwW Publishing on the Companies House website. The full name of the company had been registered as *Women's Words Written*. The registered address was Thistle Street, Edinburgh, the listed directors were Leo Monkton, Caroline Monkton and Mhairi Beaton. Rose whistled. Caroline had kept that quiet. WwW looked like it would be a direct competitor to Maypole. She printed out the listing and pinned it to the board. She checked the time; she could easily get to the registered address before five..

Thistle was a narrow cobbled street running parallel to George Street and Princess Street. With boutique shops, independent pubs, and restaurants, the location was popular with tourists and locals. WwW's registered office was above Sally's Up North, a hair salon. Rose pressed the bell and waited, there was no answer. She stepped back to look up at the window. The blind was half down and the cactus plant suspended in the middle of the window looked as if it was thriving, with spectacular pink flowers in full bloom. Her mother had had one of those plants, she'd told Rose they were impossible to kill and could be neglected, although the one Rose bought when she first left home had died within a year.

Rose wandered into the hairdressers. 'Can I help you?' A woman wearing a black apron with a pink and blue pixie cut bobbed up from behind the counter.

'I'm here to collect something from the publishers' offices above. I'm a friend of one of the owners, Caroline;

58

she said the salon had a spare key? There's been a tragic accident.'

The woman blinked slowly and gazed at Rose through her long false eyelashes.

Rose held her nerve, hoping her hunch was right. 'Are you Sally?'

'Yeah. Are you talking about what happened to Mhairi? She was lovely. One of my favourite customers.' She stood still as a statue while a tear rolled down her cheek and plopped onto the counter. Sniffing loudly she used the sleeve of her top to wipe the moisture from her face. 'I don't have a key to upstairs, I've no idea why anyone thought I did. The agents' offices are just across the road, above the sandwich shop. They have spare keys to all the properties they rent out.'.

'Thanks. I'll try there. How well did you know Mhairi, just as a customer?'

'Yeah, pretty much.' The woman stopped herself abruptly.

'Right. But if there's anything you do know, anything that might help her friends and family. I mean it's been a huge shock to everyone.'

'You'd be better off talking to that Leo. He's the one who broke her heart, ran off with Mhairi's so-called best friend.'

'Are you saying that Mhairi and Leo were an item?'

The woman nodded. 'He broke it off three months ago, when his engagement was announced. Mhairi cried buckets, she had no idea he was going behind her back, sleeping with Belinda.'

Rose frowned. 'That sounds pretty mean, especially considering that Mhairi was part of Belinda's wedding party. I met her, at the hen night.'

Sally flushed. 'I need to get back to my customer. Sorry.'

'Of course, sorry I interrupted you. But if you think of anything else, would you mind giving me a ring?' She pulled out a business card.

'Why should I talk to you?'

'I catered the hen party, I found Belinda's body. Her sister asked me to find out anything I could, to help the police catch whoever killed her.' Rose placed the business card on top of the counter. 'It sounds like Mhairi was a really good person,' she said as she turned to leave and wondered why Sally hadn't mentioned the murder, or that she had been booked as hairdresser for the wedding party.

# Chapter Eight

Rose made her way back to Morrison Street. She had a mammoth amount of work to do for the new shop Muffins On The Forth; but her head was full thinking about the information she had gleaned from the hairdresser.

Trixie and Rob were both in the kitchen when she arrived.

'Och Rose, ye came at the rit time. I'm lovin this new chocolate, cream cheese an chilli recipe.' Trixie pointed to a fresh batch of muffins filled with cream cheese and topped with a dark cocoa glaze.

'Oh yumm, they do look good. Did you get a chance to try out any of the other recipes?'

'Yep, so far so guid. Nae one fail so far and the gluten free ginger cake is braw.'

Rob nodded enthusiastically. 'Agreed,' he said, biting into one of the chocolate muffins. 'You'll need to pay me danger money for all this tasting I'm doing, my waistline is expanding. Ian said there'll soon be too much of me to love.'

Rose laughed. 'You do know tasting doesn't equate to whole muffins and slices of cake you idiot!'

Rob chuckled. '*Idiot*, well that's nice I must say. What an ingrate.'

'I have a ton of paperwork to do for the new shop, which is why I came in, but as you're both here, if you've finished the test baking, do you mind if I talk to you about Belinda's murder?' Rose put up her hands, 'I'm not asking either of you to get involved, but there are a few things that don't make sense.'

'Sure,' said Rob.

'Trixie?'

'Ah'm nae really wantin' tae help ye Rose, but ah can listen, if ye think it will help.'

Rose filled them both in about what the hairdresser had told her. 'Which means either Belinda lied to Amanda about when she met Leo, or Amanda knew about Mhairi and Leo but didn't tell Belinda that Leo and Mhairi were an item. I can't see why Mhairi would not have told Belinda she was dating Leo when she'd told her hairdresser she was in love with him.'

'Wait, when the engagement was announced, Leo was still seeing Mhairi and she had no idea he was seeing Belinda?' Rob asked. 'He played both women?'

'That's what the hairdresser said.'

'Nae, that wee Belinda knew Leo was seeing Mhairi and decided to scoop him for hersel,' said Trixie.

'You could be right, Trixie. And then there's the publishing deal. The letter from WwW to Belinda was dated a month after the company was registered, either Belinda had no idea who was behind WwW or, if she did, it could confirm that Belinda lied to Amanda.'

'Or Amanda's been lying tae ye all along. Ye mentioned that ye felt Amanda was still keepin' a secret, remember. And wha' aboot Hoffman?'

'Anthony doesn't think Belinda's murder has anything to do with him. He's given a whole bunch of information to the police and he's trying to find out what Hoffman is doing back in Edinburgh.

'If Hoffman's here, why haven't the police arrested him?' said Rob.

'Same reason he got away with murder in the first place. Friends in high places.'

Trixie shook her head and shivered. 'Aww just thinkin' aboot him makes ma blood run cold. He's an evil monster. Hae ye asked Amanda aboot anything the hairdresser told ye?'

'No, I came straight here. Talking to Amanda is next on my list. I'm not looking forward to it.'

'Want me to come wi' ye again?' asked Trixie.

'No, you're good. I'm hoping to meet her somewhere neutral; it'll be easier if she has been lying all along and we end up in a confrontation.'

'But if she's involved why would she have asked you to help her?' Rob scratched his head and looked puzzled.

'Muddy the waters? Maybe she didn't realise how seriously I would take it, once I agreed to help.'

'So you are thinking she had something to do with Belinda's death?'

'All I know is that someone who was locked in the house that night was responsible and Amanda is holding something back. Something else happened that night.'

'Well Mhairi has a motive; she was the jilted lover. Then she killed herself because of what she'd done. Are you going to tell Hickson what the hairdresser told you?'

'I should. Only fair. Your theory, it's nice and neat and the police might think that too. I just have a feeling that it couldn't have been Mhairi, but I don't know why.'

'Ah do,' said Trixie, 'well ah think ah do.'

Rose and Rob turned to look at Trixie.

'The girls hae been friends fir years, since they were weans. An we all saw them at the party, they were pals. There was hee haw to suggest there were hard feelings, which ah have to say ah would hae had if my so called friend treated me that way. So either Mhairi is a good actor or, yer gut feelin' is right Rose. An, from past experience, ah'd alway's go wi' that.'

Rose smiled, 'Thanks Trixie, not exactly scientific, but you're right, they did still appear to be close, despite Leo.' Rose could see the two women in her mind's eye. They were embracing each other after dancing together and later, when she thought about where Belinda was sitting it was usually next to Mhairi. In fact Belinda was more often with Mhairi than she was with Amanda, who'd arranged everything, especially at the end. The two women had been almost glued at the hip. Rose wrote down a list of the locations and times where she had seen Mhairi and Belinda together. She repeated the list with the names of the other women, including Amanda. She passed her notes to Rob and Trixie. 'Is this what you both remember?'

They both checked the list and nodded. 'What about the women who weren't staying at the house, why not include them?'

'Och, she's already said why, Rob, ye numpty. The murderer was staying in the hoose. My vote is for the American woman.'

Rose wrinkled her nose and finished the mug of tea. She looked back at the list she'd made. Caroline hadn't been particularly friendly towards anyone. As a director of WwW she must have been lying about why Leo was in the UK and when she said she hadn't known about Belinda before the engagement, but that didn't make her a murderer. 'The thing that's bugging me most is how Belinda ended up in the garden naked when she went upstairs with everyone else. Once I figure that out, I'll be able to work out who killed her.'

Rob and Trixie exchanged glances as Rose got up from the table and gathered up the mugs. Rob put his hand over Trixie's. 'We'll not stop her now.'

'Tha's wit worries me,' said Trixie.

Rose spent the following day making maps and going over everything again. By the time she went to bed she had a feeling that she was beginning to figure out just how Belinda could have ended up back in the garden.

# Chapter Nine

But the following day changed everything that Rose thought she knew. She was scrolling through her phone when she saw the click bait for a national newspaper- *Ill Fated Lovers in Tragic Death Triangle*. Below the headline was a picture of Belinda, Mhairi and Leo. She clicked on the article.

*Leo Monkton 31, fiancé of murdered bride Belinda Sanderson 25 and former lover of suicide victim Mhairi Beaton 26, fell to his death yesterday evening. The fatal accident happened at Camden Underground, on the Northern Line. Passengers on the crowded platform were shocked when Monkton appeared to stumble and then fall when the incoming train approached. 'He wasn't a jumper' said one witness while another said she thought he was drunk or high because of the way he was swaying unsteadily on his feet before the train arrived.*

Rose turned on the television news channel, but they were concentrating on the politics of the day and what the new year would bring economically. It was December 30th; six days had passed since she'd found Belinda's body in the small hours of Christmas Eve. She had called Leo for the last four of them. If only she hadn't been in the shower the one time he'd called her back. Caroline had said she was travelling to London today, to spend New Year with him. Who or what had taken him to Camden, Rose mused. Leo lived in Battersea, south of the river. And the publishing imprint, where he worked, was in Holborn, which is served by the Central and Piccadilly lines.

Rose studied the boards on the wall behind the couch and placed a yellow post-it note underneath the photos of Belinda and Mhairi with the date and time of Leo's death. She then drew a circle and mapped in the area Leo would have travelled between, from Battersea to Holborn and then to Camden Town. According to the report in the press he died at just after eight in the evening. She tapped her pen against the board, he could have been meeting friends there or maybe he had a late business meeting. The description by the witness who had seen him swaying, because he was drunk or high, sounded unlikely from what she knew about Leo so far. If he was drunk he would have been able to afford a taxi to take him home or used an Uber. She was about to phone Caroline when her phone rang. It was DCI Hickson.

'I'm guessing you've heard the news by now, that Leo is dead?'

'Yes, I was just ...'

The DCI interrupted her. 'And when were you going to tell me about visiting a certain hairdresser yesterday?'

'Sorry, I meant to do that last night, I got caught up in paperwork for my new shop and it was after ten at night by the time I was finished. I was going to speak to you today. You can ask Rob and Trixie, I ...'

'Rose, when I asked you to map out that evening Belinda was murdered, it was because I respected your thought process. What you did yesterday and not immediately telling me what you were up to is tantamount to interfering in a police investigation. Do you understand me?'

'Yes. I know I should have called you straight away. Do you think ... well, Leo, that it wasn't an accident.'

'*Accident* is the official line, I have no reason to think otherwise, unless he really did jump. If you have any other ideas I strongly urge you to stay out of it unless you have evidence. The Met won't take kindly to anyone stirring things up. I need you to go to the police station today to make a statement.'

'A statement?'

'Yes, I need a paper trail about yesterday Rose. My boss is, let's just say you're lucky you weren't in earshot at the briefing. I doubt we'll be ordering any more muffins for meetings anytime soon. You do realise you could still be considered a suspect for Belinda's murder.'

Rose's stomach churned. She felt as if she had been kicked, her normally quick mind went blank. `Umm no, but of course, I suppose because I found the body ... Why did that hairdresser call you?'

'She called the station and spoke to Jones. You made her suspicious, all the questions and then you asked her to call you. We already knew that Leo, his sister and Mhairi were directors of WwW Publishing.'

'I'll come down to the station later.'

'I'm out of town on another case. You can speak to Jones, he'll be expecting you.'

Rose clicked off the call. She stared out of the window for several minutes, and then phoned Amanda.

.oOo.

The coffee shop at the other end of Morrison was busy with visitors for the Hogmanay celebrations. Edinburgh had become a destination for international revellers wanting to celebrate the New Year. Amanda looked somewhat better than when Rose had last seen her, at least she wasn't wearing pyjamas and she'd combed her hair. Her eyes were puffy from fresh crying.

'I can't believe it, Rose. All three of them, in less than a week. All dead.'

Rose reached her hand across the table. 'I'm so sorry.'

'You wanted me to bring Belinda's journal, but the police must still have it. It's not in the box of things they returned. Although I don't remember giving the journal to them.'

'But you said Belinda had it at the house you rented for the hen party?'

'Yes, we were laughing about her entry from the week before - she shared what she'd written about becoming a bride. It was very Jane Austen, which wasn't Belinda's reality.'

'Although, of course, what happened between Leo and Mhairi could be considered very Jane Austen, the deception I mean.'

'What are you talking about? The papers made all that up. Mhairi and Leo weren't lovers. I don't know who told them they were, but if I get hold of them. God some people are cruel and sick aren't they?' Amanda's face flushed with anger.

Rose leaned in, 'Are you sure, because yesterday, before Leo died, well … it doesn't matter who, but someone told me about Leo and Mhairi.'

'It's impossible. Who told you ? You saw them both at the hen party. Do you really think they would have been so close with each other if Leo had been cheating on Mhairi with Belinda, and Mhairi found out?'

'Did you know that Leo, Mhairi and Leo's sister were behind WwW, the publishing company who offered Belinda a publishing deal for her book? The same book that was being published by the imprint Leo worked for, who'd threatened to sue Belinda?'

'What? No!' Amanda slumped in her chair, open mouthed and glared at Rose.

Rose pulled out her notebook and wrote: *journal, earrings, clothing, key, business card. Woman in baseball cap.*

'What are you writing?'

Rose showed her the list. 'It's always the small things that don't seem important that bother me. Although the existence of the woman in the baseball cap isn't small, I grant you. For example, if you didn't give the police Belinda's journal, where is it? Where are her clothes etc. Do you see?'

'I have an idea about the key, but it would mean a trip to London if I'm right. To where Leo and Beli were living.'

Rose nodded then tilted her head to one side. 'Do you still have access to Torphichen Street? Didn't you rent the house until after Hogmanay for the London crowd?'

'They were staying on, yes. But they didn't stay there. They've all gone back down south. Now they want me to refund them the money they contributed for the extra nights.'

'Who owns it by the way?'

'A friend of Sinead's Dad. He's a property developer who has several Airbnb, and holiday homes in the UK and Europe. If it's important I'll ping you with the details.' Amanda sent Rose a text with the name of the business and contact information. The address was listed as Thistle Street, Edinburgh, it was the same company that managed WwW and Sally's hair salon.

'Well, look at that. Curiouser and curiouser,' muttered Rose under her breath.

She forwarded the information to Anthony, along with a text.

*Any connection to Hoffman? Do they manage his property?*

'I'd like to go back to the Torphichen Street house, do you want to come?'

Amanda nodded. 'Sure.'

.oOo.

Rose spent several minutes taking photographs of the front of the house, focusing on the windows and front door. The basement had a separate entrance. Rose remembered that the patio which flowed out from the french doors on the ground level at the back of the house prevented access from the basement to the garden, except for the bin area. 'Do you have keys for the basement?'

'No, it's only used by the owner, for storage apparently.'

Rose ran down the steps. There were shutters covering the window and the glass in the door had a curtain pulled across it. 'Hmm, well he's taken care of anyone wanting to see inside. Are you ok to go back in the house?'

Amanda shrugged and pulled out the two keys for the front door. 'I'll follow you once I've turned off the alarm.'

Rose had no idea what she was looking for as she walked upstairs, but her gut told her she'd missed something on the last visit. Starting at the top of the house she opened the wardrobes and looked inside the dressers in each of the bedrooms. One of the bedrooms had an ensuite shower, the other bedrooms had washstands and shared a spacious bathroom at the back. As she walked across the varnished wood overlaid with rugs in the front bedroom she heard one of the boards creak underfoot. Rose got down on her hands and knees, lifted the draped coverings hanging over the bed and ran her hands across the floor. Her eyesight was too poor to see properly, even when she focused the torch from her phone into the dark cavernous space. She called down to Amanda to come up and help.

'But the police would have ...' Amanda protested when Rose explained what she wanted her to do.

'How did you know it was there?' Amanda exclaimed after they pushed the bed across to the wall and Rose prised open two partially cut floorboards to expose a military style backpack.

'A hunch, from that creaking board, everywhere else is so perfect, no creaks or groans which you'd expect with a house of this age. It made me think about my father's attic. One area of it creaked after the new flooring went down because he used part of the underneath for storage.'

'But I thought you said whoever was here took something from the bathroom, on the next floor down?'

'Whoever came here that morning knew about this hiding space, but they must have also been in this room. Maybe they were hiding here when they heard me come in or they also took something from this room as well as the bathroom. I think it's likely there are more secret places.'

'Probably just from here, I mean you said there wasn't anything in the bathroom. But you think the intruder was here when you arrived?'

'Pretty sure that's right because I heard the board. If it hadn't been for that and they'd waited until I went into the garden I wouldn't have known they were here. I can't ask the DCI whether they managed to find anything useful on CCTV. She said it was a blackspot. I'm no longer very popular down at the station.'

'The woman I saw running out of the house, Kyla, Neive or Sinead, which one would you pick?'

'Hand on heart, not one of them. They're just ordinary lassies, they all loved Beli. It has to have been somebody from London or someone else, someone we don't know!'

Rose bit her lip and put her hand on Amanda's shoulder. 'Come on, horrible as it is, we need to think of everyone who was here as a potential killer.'

'Including me?'

'Even me, the police suspect everyone who was here. You asked for my help, I don't think you'd have done that if you were involved, but I've been fooled before,' said Rose, remembering how she had been duped by her ex, Troy and landed up in prison for a fraud she hadn't committed. She leaned down and lifted the backpack. But even before she unzipped it, the weight already told her whatever had been hidden in there was gone.

Rose rummaged inside the pack, looking for any trace of whatever might have been kept in it then replaced it under the boards. She opened the wardrobe and dresser drawers and tapped the inside of each structure.

'What are you doing?'

'Looking for another hidey hole. I just wish I had an idea of what was being hidden. Is there any way of getting into that basement?'

Amanda shook her head. 'Both the front and back door, where the rubbish bins are kept, have multiple security locks. There's also a camera facing the back door, although it might just be for show.'

Rose pulled a face. 'Doubt it, he's gone to a lot of trouble to keep it secure.'

'Sinead's dad's a lawyer, I doubt if he'd mix with dodgy people, although Sinead is embarrassed that he does represent quite a few.'

'It's refreshing you're so innocent. You'd be shocked what so-called professionals and respectable people get up to.'

'Oh, believe me, I'm not that innocent, or naive. Where should we look next - for a hidey hole I mean?'

The two women spent the next two hours searching through the house, in cupboards, under rugs and behind pictures. They were about to give up, Rose was replacing all the pans she had emptied from under the kitchen island when she noticed a rectangular cut in the back panel. She checked the exterior, the island was at least several inches bigger on the outside. She slid a kitchen knife into where the panel was cut, then levered it until the wood gave way and the cut piece fell forward. She pulled out her camera and photographed the row of stacked gold ingots. There were twenty four of them.

'Is that a fortune?' Amanda asked when Rose showed her what she'd found.

'I would say they were worth quite a bit. Feel, it's pretty heavy for its size.'

Amanda held one of the ingots in her hand and moved it up and down, as if she were calculating the weight. 'It's more than double the weight of a new baby.'

Rose nodded. 'Yeah, so if the woman who was here was taking some of these babies, if that's what was in the back pack and under the bath, I doubt she couldn't have carried anything like this with her. From the way she moved, whatever she was carrying was pretty light. I'll call the DCI, let her know what we've found. Who knows if this has anything to do with Belinda's murder, or if we've stumbled on something else. Of course, people who invest in gold do hide it, but if it's legitimate it's usually kept in a safe or at the bank.'

Rose sent the picture of the ingots to Anthony, with a text.

*Treasure at the murder house! I'll let the DCI know; thought it might be useful in case you find any ties between the owner and Hoffman via the management company. R x*

Then she sent a message to Sinead, Kyla and Neive inviting them to meet together at her shop on Morrison Street for coffee and muffins.

# Chapter Ten

Rose wrote the date, December 30th, on a clean sheet of paper in her notebook. She'd set up a plate of freshly baked muffins on the window table ready for when Amanda and Belinda's friends were to arrive.

She looked about the shop remembering the first Christmas she'd opened. Was she right to expand to a second shop? With the inheritance from her father she could have left Trixie and Rob to run Morrison Street and moved down to Bristol, closer to Kay. Opened something there. But she knew now, she and Kay would never happen, become a couple, but she did wish they could stay friends. There'd been no texts or late night calls from Kay in New York and Rose hadn't reached out to her, since cancelling the flight on the 26th. She was deep in thought when she heard a tap on the window. It was Anthony.

'What are you doing here?' he asked as she unlocked the door and beckoned him inside, out of the frozen rain. The snowfall had turned to slush and the pavements were a mess of brown ice and puddles.

'I'm meeting the women who were at the hen party, what about you? This isn't your neck of the woods, but it's good to see you.'

Anthony smiled and leaned in to give her a hug.

'What? Come on spill!' Rose demanded.

'I'm probably being silly and getting ahead of myself but...'

'Hoffman?' Rose interrupted.

Anthony put up his hand to stop her. 'No, it's, well it's more personal than that, I was going to tell you the other day, but after you told me about Kay, it didn't feel right to say that I've err, well I've met someone.' He flushed as he spoke.' We've met a couple of times for a drink and ... I'

'Jings, you're going on a date! You're very smart for lunch, so I'm thinking it might be a long date, evening too?'

Anthony nodded. The flush deepened, to match the silk tie he was wearing. 'I'm early, and I thought I'd... Look, what do you think?' Anthony pulled a blue bag from his coat pocket and took out a small box. The silver earrings were cast into a delicate flower shape with a tiny crystal in the centre. Too much? '

'No. They're beautiful, she's a lucky woman, but who is she?'

'Her name is Cathy, her husband died five years ago. We met on Christmas Day; she was one of the waifs and strays.'

'I'm happy for you, and if you're already buying earrings, I'd say it was serious. Take your own advice and please be careful.'

Anthony smiled and shuffled awkwardly. 'It's been a long time. I'm trying not to scare her off, but I don't know how to be cool. And, I promise I haven't taken my eye off things regarding Hoffman. Your text, I didn't reply but it gave me an idea. I'll contact you tomorrow.'

Rose gave him a hug. Anthony had just left when the bell to the shop door jangled. The three women from the hen party arrived together, stamping off their wet boots and freeing their hair from under thick winter coat hoods.

'Come in and get warm, it's baltic out there.' Rose indicated the table with the muffins and took their orders for tea and coffee.

'Isn't Amanda coming?' Neive asked.

'Yes, she'll be along too.' Rose set the steaming mugs on the table and opened her notebook. 'I know you've gone over everything that happened the night Belinda was killed with the police. Because I was still in the kitchen and out on the patio when you'd all gone to bed, I'm trying to figure out why I didn't see or hear anyone come back down. And as we're all under the eye of DCI Hickson, I thought sharing what each of us saw or heard might be useful.'

All three women exchanged glances, then nodded. Rose could see from their response she'd played her part well so far, but the message they'd exchanged when they looked at each other hadn't escaped her notice. She was an interloper. Rose unfolded a large sheet of paper onto which she'd drawn a map of the house. She had shaded in the basement and the attic spaces, and named all the rooms. Ground Floor: hallway, two piece bathroom, front sitting room, open plan kitchen with seating, atrium/dining room and exit to the patio, bedroom/study and ensuite. Middle Floor: master bedroom and ensuite (Belinda and Amanda), front bedroom (Caroline), front bedroom (Mhairi), bathroom and small rear bedroom (made up for a London guest). Top Floor: bathroom, front bedroom one with ensuite (?), front bedroom two (?), rear bedroom three (?). 'You three were all on the top floor?'

'Yes,' Neive said. 'I was in the bedroom at the back, Sinead was in the ensuite and Kyla was in the other front bedroom.'

Rose glanced up, to look at Sinead's response. She had been staying in the room where they had found the backpack and it was a friend of her fathers who owned the house. But nothing in Sinead's demeanour indicated she was bothered by Rose knowing which room she'd had. 'OK, can each of you go over what happened once you'd gone upstairs, I mean were the curtains still open, did you hear anything that, now you think about it, sounded odd or out of place?'

'The only thing I can remember after all that booze is wanting to pee really badly. Caroline had come upstairs to our bathroom and Sinead was in the shower in her ensuite,' said Kyla. 'I'm afraid I told Caroline what I thought of her when she came out. She'd been getting my goat all evening; she was so stuck up and rude.'

'Haha yeah, I remember thinking, go Kyla,' said Neive.

'But you didn't come back downstairs to use the ground floor toilet in the hallway?'

'God no, I'd not have made it, I had to...' she flushed 'improvise, I used the waste bin in my bedroom, and emptied it down the sink.'

Neive and Sinead were roaring with laughter when Amanda arrived. 'What did I miss?'

'Ah, stop it, will you? I was desperate!' Kyla protested as Sinead mimed the story and told Amanda the cause of the laughter.

Watching the women together, how close, and comfortable they were with each other, Rose found it hard to imagine that any of them could have had anything to do with Belinda's murder, but she still had a niggling thought, the exchanged glances before anyone confirmed any of her questions told her they were checking in with each other. When they had settled down Rose tried to open up the conversation again, but no one claimed to remember hearing or seeing anything before they went to bed. After they left, Rose sighed and examined the layout of the house as she had drawn it. The exit to the basement from within the main house had been closed off and access to the attic was through a small panel in the ceiling of the hallway on the upper landing. Rose was convinced there were still other hidey holes. Unless someone had accessed the basement, hidden in the summerhouse or leapt over one of the walls that surrounded the garden, Belinda's murderer had to have been Mhairi or one of the women she had just shared coffee and muffins with. As she folded up her drawing of the house, she realised what else had bothered her. It was the downstairs bathroom.

Rose sent a text to Amanda. *I need to get back inside Torphichen, any chance you could meet me there?*

Amanda texted back. *?*

*I'll explain when I see you. The downstairs bathroom, like the island in the kitchen - it's bigger on the outside!*

*What? Omw!*

.oOo.

'Look,' Rose pointed to the panelled mirrored wall on one side of the two piece bathroom, off the main hallway. 'This would have been where the original stairs were, to access the basement. But what if they are still here, just hidden,' she said, pushing and tapping on the glass panels.

'Rose, please don't break the glass, I can't afford to…' Amanda's voice trailed off when the middle glass panel started to slide backwards and tuck behind. The tracking was masterfully done, like an invisible seam, you only knew it was there when you looked for it. As the panel moved a cavernous dark hole appeared in the floor. Rose peered down. A metal loft ladder had been fixed to the joist. She pressed the torch app on her phone and gingerly started to climb down.

'What do you see?' Amanda shouted from above as she watched Rose move away from the ladder.

'I'm going to take pictures, wait there and listen, just in case someone saw us come in.' Rose turned on a light switch which flooded the room with fluorescence by four long tubes suspended from the ceiling. A large table stood in the middle of the floor; a bank of cabinets stood against the furthest wall with three large printing machines pushed against the opposite wall. A bank of three computer stations and a laptop filled the back wall, next to the solid wooden back door. Rose opened one of the cabinets. Inside she found a stack of different papers, bundles of US dollar bills, Russian rubles, 500 euro notes, banknotes from the UK, and Australia. In another of the cabinets there were different coloured passport covers, with papers and a multitude of tools needed to create documents. Rose shivered, her ex, Troy, had been a master of creating fraudulent documents.

She photographed her find and made her way to the front of the basement. Both the rooms were locked. There was a toilet which needed a good clean and a sink with plates, mugs and cutlery soaking in minging water. The kettle and microwave were both ancient and filthy.

Rose had just climbed back up the ladder when she heard the sirens outside. Within seconds the police were banging on the front door and demanding entry. DCI Hickson was walking up the steps when Amanda opened the door.

'Why are you both here?' she demanded as Rose stood behind Amanda.

Rose indicated with her hand for the DCI to follow her. 'I was just about to call you,' she said as she held out her phone to show the DCI the photographs of what she had discovered in the basement. 'How did you know we were here?'

DCI Hickson glared grimly back at Rose, her eyes were cold and steely as she shook her head and ordered one of the officers down into the basement.

'Did you know this was here Amanda, is that why you showed Rose?'

'No, I had no idea, Rose figured it out.'

'Really, you've never seen this before, are you sure?'

'Absolutely.'

The DCI paused, she flicked her tongue around the inside of her mouth and appeared to be considering whether or not she believed Amanda.

'And the night of the murder, no one came through the basement into the house?'

Rose and Amanda looked at each other. Amanda's face was flushing, she looked as if she was about to have another panic attack.

'Breathe Amanda,' said Rose, wondering whether the DCI had a point. Had Amanda known about the basement all along?

# Chapter Eleven

'Hopefully that rules out Mhairi and the rest of us as suspects,' said Amanda as she and Rose sipped on hot chocolates at Rose's flat in Corstorphine. 'And Leo,' she added as an afterthought.

'You really had no idea about the basement?'

'No, I really didn't Rose. I panicked I could tell the DCI thought I was lying, but I swear to you, what you found today, I had no idea about how the basement connected to the house.'

'OK. About that key, you said you had an idea about what it opened?'

'Yeah, there was an old desk that Beli loved, Queen Anne. She asked me if I would store it for her when she and Leo married, he preferred modern styles and Habitat, even though the flat he owned was built in the 1800's. I suggested she sell it but she became quite upset and said she couldn't. Anyhow, she told me she'd found a lock up in Clerkenwell for cheap, someone's garage, and she was storing her stuff there for the time being.'

'And the police don't know about the lock-up?'

'Not yet, we'd agreed you wanted to find out what the key opened first. Remember?'

Rose nodded, although it wasn't exactly how she remembered the conversation. Amanda had said she had no idea what the key might open, now she had suddenly remembered both an old desk and a lock up. 'I could travel down tomorrow if you know the address.'

'Hogmanay? Don't you have plans?'

'I was supposed to be in New York, but...'

'That's my fault.'

'Not really, I mean I cancelled on Kay because I agreed to help you out, I was still planning to go. Or at least I thought I was, I'm not so sure now.'

'I'm not very lucky in love either. I always seem to choose the wrong man.'

'It's easily done. Do you know the address for the lock up?'

'No, I just remember she said it was a garage in Clerkenwell.'

Rose started scrolling advertisements online for lock ups in Clerkenwell. 'When did she rent it?'

Amanda shrugged.

'It's like looking for the proverbial needle in a haystack. I'll need more to go on. Most of these ads are for companies renting out storage lockers. But I could go to the flat, there might be paperwork there. I'll contact Caroline, to see about getting access.'

Rose was heading for bed when she saw the text from Anthony. *Brunch tomorrow? I may have news.*

*Heading to London at 2pm. Early brunch? 10am at Le Marché?*

*Perfect. London?*

*C u tomorrow. Will explain then.*

Rose was settled at a table in Le Marché and pouring herself coffee. 'You really have some news?' she asked as soon as Anthony arrived. 'Did your date not last as long as you hoped?'

'Hello to you too,' he grinned and waved an envelope at her. 'The date was fine but I couldn't sleep so I did a bit of digging and voilà! It turns out that our old friend Hoffman is an investor in Monkton Press, Leo's parents' business. It was a complete chance I found it, look here.' He pulled some papers out of the envelope. A record of shareholders, along with two newspaper articles.

'I don't see Hoffman's name anywhere,' said Rose as she scanned the documents. 'Oh wait, Lance Cooper!'

'And.' Anthony pointed to the newspaper article.

Rose scanned the copy underneath the photograph.

*Mr and Mrs Monkton, with their children Mark and Caroline and staff, celebrate forty years in business. A new partnership will take the company global. Monkton Press has opened offices in Russia and Australia in addition to their existing presence in Germany, New York, Los Angeles, London and Holland.*

Rose leaned in closer, the Monkton family were assembled in front of their building, flanked by a large group of people. 'I had no idea Leo had a brother.'

Anthony tapped on the image, 'Look, do you see who else is in the picture, up close and personal with Hoffman and the Monkton family?'

Rose leaned in again, 'Oh my days. That's Amanda and Sinead!'

'Hoffman has turned his face away from the camera, but that's definitely him alright.'

'Talk about six degrees of separation,' said Rose. 'Amanda deliberately lied to me about, well not about knowing Hoffman, but she claimed they hadn't seen any of the Hoffman side of the family for years. She also,' Rose put her fingers into quotation marks, '*didn't* tell me that she and Sinead were with Leo's family in New York - before she claims Belinda met Leo. It might explain why Caroline was so weird at the hen party though.'

Anthony showed her the second newspaper article.

*Monkton Press. Son shamed and arrested for fraud. Disinherited by family. "He's dead to me," claims father.*

'Harsh, I wonder why he did it?'

'You said a friend of Sinead's father rented Amanda the house. The photos you sent me yesterday from the basement, are you sure Amanda had no idea what was down there?'

Rose lifted her eyebrows, 'Honestly, at this point I don't know what to believe.''

'Look where the offices of Monkton Press are.'

'Right, of course, huh. The same countries as the notes. Rubles, Euros, Dollars and Pounds.'

'How come you're going to London?'

Rose explained about the lock up that Belinda reportedly had in Clerkenwell. 'I phoned Caroline and she asked me if I thought I could help throw any light on what had happened to her brother. The police are being less than forthcoming and, in the light of his fiancée's murder and Mhairi's suicide, told her his death was a tragic accident due to an over-consumption of alcohol. Caroline is booked to fly back to the United States on January 2nd. She's frustrated that her brother's body isn't going to be released. Her parents want Leo to be buried in the family plot in New York State, but the red tape's endless. I told her I'd do what I could to help, that maybe if we could find where the lock up is there would be answers. I'm booked on a flight to London this afternoon. I'm only planning to be there for one night.'

Anthony frowned. 'I don't like it Rose, now that we know Amanda, Sinead and Caroline were in contact with each other and with Hoffman.'

Rose drummed her fingers on the table. 'You think this is a set up?'

'I think you need to talk to DCI Hickson about all of this before you go anywhere.'

'But you've always said the reason Hoffman got away with murder last time is because he's well connected. That people at the top are protecting him. Wouldn't there be more risk in telling the police what we know?'

'I've given Hickson everything I have on Hoffman, but it doesn't appear to have made a difference yet. You may be right. In which case I'm going to have to come to London with you.'

Rose didn't protest at Anthony's suggestion; three hours later they were both fastening their seat belts, preparing to land at Heathrow.

As soon as they were inside the terminal Rose's phone pinged with a text from Caroline.

*Found an invoice with the address of the lock-up. Meet me there, rather than the flat. Pic of invoice attached.*

'Well that's very convenient isn't it.'

Rose nodded. 'I kind of thought that yesterday, when Amanda told me about the desk in a lock up. I was really hoping to see Leo's flat. Where he and Belinda were living.'

'Let's do that first, while Caroline is away waiting for you at the lock-up.'

'Wait', Rose stopped in her tracks, 'Are you suggesting we break in? You who never does anything beyond the law?'

Anthony grinned, 'I suppose retirement and the dogged pursuit of Hoffman is leading me astray.'

Rose laughed as she tucked her arm into his and they made their way to the taxi rank.

.oOo.

Leo's flat was on the second floor of a purpose built terrace called Albert Mansions. The nineteenth century building, on Albert Bridge in Battersea, overlooked Battersea Park. Rose rang the bell while Anthony walked to the end of the terrace to see if there was access via the rear of the property, but the gate was secure and too exposed to risk forcing the lock. 'I doubt anyone is going to just let us in, so you'll need to make up a good story.'

Rose was about to retort, when two women came through the front door, they were in deep discussion with each other and paid no attention to the two strangers. Rose shot her foot out to stop the door closing, then she and Anthony ducked inside and headed up the central staircase.

The door to Leo's flat was solid and fitted with two Banham locks. 'Well that's that then,' said Rose.

Anthony pulled out a ring with several keys on it from his pocket, 'Maybe not,' he said, as he slipped one of the keys into a lock. Within seconds they were both inside the flat. Anthony pressed his finger to his lips to shush Rose. 'I'll explain later,' he whispered.

The flat was well proportioned with wooden flooring. Amanda had been right about Leo's taste, despite the age of the building, the interior of the flat was a showpiece to modernist minimalism. There were no ornaments, photographs or personal belongings. The wall art was a curated collection as was the collection of cream pottery vases by a renowned ceramicist. One end of the living room was fitted with a full bookshelf. The third bedroom had been turned into a study, it too lacked personal or sentimental decoration. There were no certificates, awards or photographs on display. The two desks were bare apart from a computer. The three black filing cabinets along the side wall were all securely locked.

'Assuming Caroline found a key to the filing cabinets or the desks, it's just plausible she found the invoice she sent you the picture of, but somehow I don't think so,' said Anthony as he unfastened the first filing cabinet. It was completely empty.

'It's as if the whole place has been staged,' said Rose as they checked the rest of the cabinets and then explored the bedrooms. The beds were made up, nothing in the room was out of place. The neatly hung and folded clothing in the wardrobes and dressers were worthy of a showroom in Harvey Nichols. 'I can't believe anyone actually lived here, yet someone has to have been cleaning it. There isn't a speck of dust or a mark anywhere.'

'It doesn't look as if Caroline stayed here yesterday either. She's just sent another text, asking whether I'm lost.'

'Well I don't think we are going to find anything here do you? Tell her yes, but you're on your way now. When we get there, I'll hang back and watch, if you're alright with that.'

.oOo.

Caroline was waiting inside the lock up. The garage was in a row of others between two blocks of flats and a mini mall. Unlike the flat the interior of the garage was chaotic. There were boxes and cases and black plastic bags piled on top of each other. A desk with an inlaid leather top had been pushed to the side, surrounded by more boxes and bags.

'I'm guessing that's the desk you were looking for. It's certainly not Leo's taste. Heavens Rose, what is all this? It's not just Belinda's though, some of it belongs to Leo. Look.' She held up a brown leather attaché case. 'My father bought him this when he finished university.'

Rose nodded. 'Did you stay at the flat last night?' She watched carefully to see whether Caroline would lie to her face.

'God no, I stayed at The Hilton. We, Monkton Press, have an account. I should have done that in Edinburgh as well.'

Rose wanted to ask her about the photograph in New York, but she could tell Caroline was on edge, she'd keep that card until later. Rose climbed over the boxes towards the desk and tried the key in the top drawer. It didn't fit. She pulled on the delicate brass handle but the drawer resisted. She tried the lower drawers, but they also remained firmly closed. 'I am guessing that whatever this key opens is in here somewhere, but it'll take the rest of the day to sort through everything.'

'And I can't hang around. A friend of Daddy's has invited me to dinner tonight. Everyone is so upset about Leo and they're all being very kind. I'll have to leave you to it.'

'What's his name?'

'Who?'

'The man who you are having dinner with?'

'I didn't say it was a man, and it's none of your business.'

'Are you dining with Lance Cooper?'

Caroline's face was drained of colour. 'No, but why did you mention him?'

'Because he killed a friend of mine in Edinburgh and then he escaped with the help of some very powerful people. His real name is Hoffman, but I expect you already knew that. After all, he put a shed load of money into your family business.'

Caroline started shaking, her posture no longer upright resembled a rag doll, as she lost control of her limbs and fell in a heap on one of the black plastic bags.

Rose climbed back over to join her and waited until she pulled herself together. Her face shone with a mixture of tears and snot, her makeup smudged, badger like, across her eyes.

'That man's going to ruin my father.'

'I think it's time you were honest with me, Caroline. Why exactly did Amanda want me to cater the hen party for Belinda? And what's the connection between your family, Hoffman and Belinda's family?'

Caroline had just started to speak when the motorbike sped past, two gunshots rang out and then the sound of breaking glass; a yellow flame began to dance by the side of a box.

'Rose, Rose!' Anthony's voice was urgent as he ran around the corner, the garage was quickly shrouded in smoke as the fire took hold.

'I'm alright, but Caroline's hurt, I'm trying to get her out, don't come in,' Rose shouted back. But Anthony was already at her side, helping Rose to support Caroline's weight, and pull her from the blaze. Her head was bleeding from where the bullet had caught the side of her temple, she was falling in and out of consciousness.

# Chapter Twelve

The paramedics arrived quickly. Caroline was taken straight into surgery when they arrived at the hospital. Rose had been checked over, as had Anthony, they'd both escaped physically unscathed.

'Did you see the bike, get a number plate?'

'It all happened so fast, and I was around the side of the garage. They came in from the other end.'

'Thank God they didn't see you. They could have...'

'Stop, we're both alright; we have to hope Caroline will be as well.'

Rose chewed on her lip. 'She was about to tell me about the connection between her family, Hoffman, and Belinda's family. She said Hoffman was going to ruin her father.'

'Well I was certainly wrong wasn't I when I said there wasn't a connection. I'm really worried about your safety. He has to have known you were catering the party at the house the night Belinda was killed.'

'Yes, I think so too. Why did I get involved? Now I'm in way too deep to not carry on.'

A tall doctor of African heritage arrived and interrupted them. 'You came with Miss Monkton? Are you family?'

'No, her brother died recently. Her family lives in America.'

'The police are with her, and she's sleeping at the moment. I'm afraid I can't let you visit her until I've spoken to a relative. Do you have contact information for them?'

'No, but I know someone who does. I'll call her. Will Caroline be alright?'

'Yes, she was very lucky, it was a superficial wound in the end.'

'Which may mean whoever did this will try again,' muttered Anthony. 'Rose, I'm going to see if the police will talk to me, off the record. There have to be some advantages to being a retired policeman.'

Rose called Amanda, then Sinead but neither of them picked up. Then she called DCI Hickson and filled her in on what had happened. 'The doctor won't let me see Caroline, until he's got permission from a relative, or if she asks for me I suppose. Anthony is trying to talk to the police, we've already given them statements.'

'Again you're in the middle of things? Anthony Chatterton should have known better than to encourage you to go down to London with potential evidence.'

'Oh for goodness sake, do you know how hard he pushed to have Hoffman investigated last time? If we'd come to you with the press cuttings and information about the shares what could you have done? Talking to Caroline, trying to find out what Belinda was hiding and how their families were connected was our best shot at finding out who killed her.'

'No Rose, your best shot as you call it is keeping me informed, which is what Anthony has done by giving me the information he's already found out about Hoffman. I'll request a record of your statement from the Met and I'd appreciate you and Anthony Chatterton coming to speak to me in person as soon as you get back to Edinburgh, is that clear?'

'Yes,' muttered Rose and ended the call.

Anthony was scowling when he returned. 'Seems I'm persona non grata, how did you get on?'

'No reply from Amanda or Sinead and a ticking off from DCI Hickson. Her bite is worse than yours was.'

'Ah, she has a reputation. I did warn you she was known as the ice queen before you two first met.'

'She wants to see both of us when we get back to Edinburgh.'

.oOo.

Rose and Anthony left the hospital an hour later and checked into a hotel. The New Year was four hours away. Caroline had regained consciousness but neither the police or medical staff would allow Rose a visit. She was writing up the event in her notebook and studying the various maps she'd made when Amanda returned her call.

'Sorry Rose, I didn't have a chance to call you back earlier. How's Caroline?'

'Why don't you tell me, Amanda?'

'What?'

Rose paused. 'Are you with Sinead?'

'Yes, and Kyla, we're just having a quiet Hogmanay at my flat.'

'Tell me again how you and Sinead didn't know Caroline or Leo, that you had no idea of any connection to Olifer Hoffman alias Lance Cooper.'

Amanda sighed. 'I should have realised you would find out. OK, I'll tell you everything. Sinead and I were on holiday. Her father knew someone who knew someone blah blah and we ended up invited to a party with Mark. His family were celebrating an anniversary for their business. I had no idea that my great uncle was going to be there. I told you we hadn't had any contact with that side of the family since before my parents died. By the time Belinda met Leo, his brother Mark was in prison.'

'So why pretend you didn't know Leo's family?'

'Because... because Sinead and I did something really stupid after the party and we were arrested. Caroline bailed us out and we were let off with a caution. I'm not even sure I'll ever be able to travel back to the USA. I'm not proud of it and it has nothing to do with anything now. But we promised Caroline not to stay in touch. She was as shocked as I was that of all the people in the world Leo met Belinda and announced they were getting married.'

'So that's why she was so cool with everyone at the hen party.'

'I was surprised she actually agreed to come, let alone stay at the house, but it's also why Leo's parents didn't come over. They were against the match, because of me. I couldn't tell Belinda that. How's Caroline?

'She's in hospital and the doctor won't let me see her until he's spoken with her parents, although I'm sure the police have made contact with them by now.'

'What doctor, what's happened?'

Rose described the events of that afternoon and what Caroline had said about Hoffman.

'That man is just evil. I know he stole my mother's inheritance, that's why he and my parents fell out.'

.oOo.

Rose slept badly, she needed to get back to Edinburgh. The temptation from the mini bar in the hotel bedroom, to numb the trauma of what had happened earlier, almost overpowered her. She'd reached out to Rob in the early hours. He'd supported her via texts and phone calls and she'd managed to stay sober. She had just woken up when her phone pinged with a text from Rob.

*Get yourself on a plane or get a train. I'll meet you. I'm staying over at yours too. No arguments!*

*I'm sorry I ruined your celebrations. I'm OK now.*

*Rose, just get yourself back here. Leave the London end to Anthony. Trixie is organising scran and she's bringing it to yours. Let's start the new year right.*

Rose smiled at her phone as she read the text. 'The pupil has become the master,' she said to herself; remembering how she had supported Rob in his fight for sobriety on a different new year, not so long ago. It was still dark, 6am. She doubted Anthony would be awake and she couldn't just take off without talking to him. She only now realised that she'd managed to ruin whatever plans he had had for the New Year by accepting his offer to travel to London with her. She hoped the woman he had fallen for would understand.

Her phone pinged again. This time with a text from Caroline.

*I'm leaving the hospital today. I'm booked on a flight home tomorrow and the doctor is fine with me travelling, but he wants to see me for a last check over. We should talk if you're still in London. I expect to be discharged from here by noon, and I'll go straight to The Hilton.*

97

Rose checked flights back to Edinburgh and booked two seats on the 12.30. That would give her enough time to see Caroline and get out to the airport. She ordered a room service breakfast for Anthony for 8am and pinged him a text with the flight details. *C U @ heathrow.*

Caroline looked well for a woman who'd literally dodged a bullet, less than twenty four hours earlier.

'Ya know, everybody raves about the NHS but the food, oh my god … no wonder you have a bed blocking problem. The longer you stay, the sicker you get and darn it, I'm even paying to be here.'

'You're in good spirits considering…'

'Yeah, considering the uncle of the woman who was going to be my sister in law tried to murder me.'

'Well we don't know that. But if it was him, and if he was responsible for killing your brother, I don't understand why Belinda was murdered.'

'Go figure. He's a loon. Didn't you say that he murdered his half brother?'

'When?'

'Huh?'

'When did I tell you that?'

'What do you mean?'

Rose didn't reply. She knew she hadn't told Caroline that Hoffman had killed Chris. So who had?

'How did someone know you'd be at the lock up? Did the police check your phone for a tracking device?'

'Yeah, but nothing.'

'So we have no idea if it was you, me or just destroying the contents of the garage they were after.'

'Well that's comforting and one of the reasons I want to high tail it out of here. I'd like to live to at least the biblical three score and ten without someone taking me down.'

'Amanda told me how you'd met before. According to her, Hoffman stole her mother's inheritance. When she saw him at the family party in New York she had no idea about the connection to your family.'

'Yeah, it was weird, when he was introduced as Lance Cooper her face gave it away. I knew something was up. He was pretty shocked to see her too. It was certainly a game of chicken that day, both of them avoiding each other. Until my dad decides he wants to have a couple of pretty girls in the photograph and insists Amanda and Sinead are front and centre with the family and their new investor.'

Rose shook her head. 'It really is a small world isn't it.'

'I guess she told you what happened later?'

'No details, just that she was arrested, her and Sinead.'

Caroline rolled her eyes, 'I guess we can all go nuts and experiment at twenty one; they were lucky neither of them died and Mark told me what had happened and not my parents.'

'Do you ever talk, you and your brother Mark?'

'No, he chose that life, he could have had everything.' Caroline's face flushed and she clenched her jaw, while blinking back tears.

Rose recognised the emotion, the pain and anger that went with thinking about someone you had once loved who betrayed you. She looked down and checked her phone. Anthony had sent a text thanking her for breakfast and booking the flights. His words were formal, restrained. She knew he wouldn't be happy that she'd taken herself off to see Caroline without him.

.oOo.

'You're mad with me … sorry,' Rose said as she sidled into the seat next to him at the gate.

He put down the paper and pointed to the headline. 'It's not going to be long before your name is out there in the press as one of the potential victims.'

'I'm sure I wasn't, in fact, if whoever it was had intended to kill either one of us, we would be dead, it feels like smoke and mirrors in a magic act. A distraction from what's really going on.'

Anthony shook his head. 'A pretty serious illusion, I don't think so,'

Rose pulled out her notebook and showed him the map she'd made the night before, after she'd talked to Amanda, before her own gremlins came to taunt her.

She'd written Hoffman Investor and Hoffman Relative on the left side of the page. Then in small circles, filling the rest of the page, she'd written Caroline, the Monkton parents, Leo, Amanda, Belinda and Sinead, as if they were all individual islands.

'What about Sinead's father, or his friend who owns the house, where you found the document lab.'

Second map - look.' Rose turned over the page. She had re-listed all the names of the guests in the house around the edge of the page, but she had placed Sinead + Dad and Amanda in the centre inside a triangle. 'Sinead's father is the connection to the Monkton's. I think you were right the first time, Belinda's death has nothing to do with Hoffman.'

.oOo.

100

DCI Hickson was on her way out of the police station when they arrived. 'There's been a fire, at Torphichen Street. Don't go anywhere until I get back.'

'Can't we come, we can talk on the way, tell you about what happened in London? I have some ideas.'

'I'm sure you do, but right now you need to let me do my job.'

Anthony put his arm on Rose's shoulder as the DCI swept out of the station followed by her junior. 'If only she'd listen, I...'

Rose plonked herself down on one of the seats in the waiting area and sent a text to Rob and Trixie to let them know she was back in Edinburgh and would see them soon. Anthony sat beside her.

*Trixie has made a feast. There's enough for Anthony, if he wants. Text me once you're done with the police.*

Two hours later, Trixie, Rose, Anthony and Rob were tucking into spicy carrot soup, savoury muffins, slabs of cheese, salad and mince pies at Rose's flat in Corstorphine.

'Why didn't she tell me that she was struggling with drinking last night?' Anthony said as he and Trixie sorted the dirty dishes in the kitchen and left Rob to talk to Rose.

'She wouldnae, ye've nae been where she wis in her heed,' said Trixie. 'But for all that, yer a good pal, an she kens it.'

'As are you Trixie, and soon to be running your own shop. Well done.'

'Ah, it's all down tae Rose. If she hadnae believed in me...' Trixie smiled and reached over for the kettle. 'Let's nae get maudlin, coffee?'

'So how do the police think the fire at Tophichen started?' asked Rob as Trixie served the strong coffee.

Rose shrugged. 'Hickson isn't about to share any information with me now, nor with...' She bobbed her head towards Anthony. 'I have an idea, look.' Rose pulled out the two maps she'd shown Anthony before and pinned them onto the boards behind her sofa.

'Tell me again why you think Hoffman had nothing to do with Belinda's murder?'

'It's like the fires and that amateur drive by yesterday, they're red herrings, that distract from whatever is really going on, take us down rabbit holes for things that aren't there. The connection between Hoffman and Belinda's family is one. The fact that he's in Edinburgh and was at that party in New York, when Amanda and Sinead were there, is a coincidence.'

'I'm not buying that theory I'm afraid. I don't believe in coincidences. All my years as a policeman have taught me, if there's a connection, however frail, it's there for a reason.'

'Ay, that makes sense,' Trixe said, nodding.

'But remember, Hoffman alias Lance Cooper is good at hiding in plain sight. This is drawing attention to him. That's not how he operates.'

'Unless...,' Anthony paused.

'What?'

'It's just a thought. And, I need to go anyway. You sure you'll be alright Rose?'

'Don't worry, I have these two on my case,' Rose replied, gesturing towards Rob and Trixie.

# Chapter Thirteen

The following morning Rose rode her e-bike via Torphichen Street, before going to the shop on Morrison to prep for re-opening.

The house was once more taped off with yellow police tape. The outside of the building looked unscathed but the upper windows had been boarded up; the shutters on the ground floor living room were closed and didn't appear damaged. Rose tilted her head and thought about the interior of the upper floor where she had found the backpack. Whoever set the fire had targeted the upper floor, the fire hadn't appeared to spread to either the ground floor or the basement. She checked her watch, Caroline would already be en route to the USA. Her journey to London, and the fire at the lock up, felt like a wild goose chase.

Later that morning, while she was blending the spices for the banana curry muffins, she had an idea. She reached for her phone to call DCI Hickson. But the DCI didn't answer; Rose decided not to leave a message. The police would need evidence before they could act officially anyway. She rang Edinburgh airport.

It took almost half an hour to get through to customer services, but the call proved fruitful. Rose chuckled, she had always been good at mimicking accents, but she hadn't successfully fooled anyone that she was an American before. Rose continued prepping the muffins and soon the kitchen was filled with a pungent aroma from the test batch of the featured muffin for January. While the muffins were baking she scrolled through some news sites on her phone. Then she sent a text to Amanda, Neive, Sinead and Kyla.

*Hi, r u busy? I have a couple of ideas I'd like to chat about plus I need taste testers for new muffins, can I tempt you over?*

She tapped her foot on the floor as she waited to see which of the women would reply first. It was Kyla.

*Sorry Rose, out of town*

*Hiya Rose, can't come today. Call me later though. A x*

*Really busy, sorry. N :(*

The final text, a few minutes later, was from Sinead.

*At my parents, not free today. Sorry.*

Rose smiled and wished she could see the flurry of texts she presumed were now pinging back and forth between the four women as she went out to buy a copy of the major nationals.

Belinda's death, Mhairi's suicide and Leo's accident were no longer headline news. The press had already lost interest in the London fire and gunshot incident. Rose found the story that had captured her interest online. An update about a court case; the perpetrator had skipped bail. The drawing from the original trial depicted a fair haired bearded man in his early thirties, but the photograph in another paper showed the perpetrator as clean shaven, with cropped dark hair. She had seen that face in a photograph before, and recently. Rose tapped the picture with her pen and tore out the articles to post on her map boards when she got back to the flat.

'Och, smells amazin' in here Rose!' Trixie said, as she wiped her boots on the mat in the doorway of the shop. It had started snowing again, but the temperature was too warm for it to settle. 'Ye happy wi' the recipe?'

'Kind of, it's loaded in terms of calories and it's sweeter than I wanted. I'm wondering if yoghurt would be better than the condensed milk. I've just put in another batch to try it out. But the flavour is good.'

Trixie cut one of the sample muffins in half and tried it. 'Mmmm, love it, dinnae change a thing. Wha's this?' Trixie asked, pointing to the newspaper clippings.

'Not sure, does that man look familiar to you?'

'Naw. Who is he?'

Rose shook her head and shrugged. 'I was hoping that Amanda or one of the friends would recognise the picture, but none of them were *free* to come over.' Rose put her fingers up to suggest inverted commas when she said the word free.'

'Well it is still the holidays.'

Rose lifted her eyebrows.

'Och, yer so funny. Not! Leave it Rose, I hate to think wha' could hae happened in London toon.'

'That second batch is about done, let's just concentrate on getting the baking right for now.'

Trixie organised her station and had just begun a spicy shortbread dough when Rob arrived. 'This was just delivered, who does it belong to?' He held up a green backpack, it was identical to the one Rose had found at the Torphichen Street house.

'Oh that was speedy,' said Rose. Let's go through to the shop and see.'

Trixie followed Rose out of the kitchen carrying a plate of muffins Rose had baked earlier. 'Tea?'

Rob nodded. Rose donned plastic gloves and opened the backpack; she took out a plastic grocery bag. Inside the plastic bag were three Christmas paper wrapped parcels. The wrapping was untidy and none of the parcels bore a label. Rose peeled open the tape and unwrapped the first parcel. There was no mistaking the green sparkly top Belinda had worn at the hen party.

Trixie gasped, dropping the tray of mugs she yelped as the boiling liquid made contact, splashing back against her legs. Rose rushed into the kitchen to grab a cold wet cloth.

When Trixie was settled, and the burns tended to, Rob made a pot of fresh tea. Rose took a photograph of the parcels and attached it to a message for the DCI. 'She's not going to thank me, but at least I'm keeping her in the loop.'

'So, how on earth did you find the bag?' Rob demanded.

'Whoever broke into Torphichen on the morning I was there stole something, I knew from the way they moved, it wasn't heavy, so not gold ingots. Belinda's clothing was still missing. I put two and two together.'

'And made five! But how did you guess they were hidden at the airport in a backpack?'

'The backpack we found upstairs is a military grade American brand, it's pretty unique and expensive. If there hadn't been a backpack at the airport I was going to try Waverley, then the bus station, but airports averagely deal with more lost luggage than train and bus stations. No one would suspect a backpack of presents contained a murdered woman's clothing. Another few weeks without a claimant, the pack would have been destroyed, along with Belinda's clothing.

'But whoever took it could hae just dumped it in a bin,' said Trixie.

'Exactly. Except have you noticed that everything that's happened, Belinda's murder, the way she was posed by the hot tub, the fire and the shots in London where neither Caroline or I were really hurt, Mhairi's suicide and Leo's accident, even the fire at Torphichen seemed controlled. Everything appears staged, as if what was happening was in a film, or a play...'

'Or in a book,' said Trixie.

'And Belinda was a writer,' said Rob.

'Steamy romance, yes. And there's another thing, remember that photograph of Belinda that appeared in a national newspaper after she was murdered, the one with the scarf? The way that was taken, as if they were posing? She was on a photo shoot, but that wasn't part of the professional portfolio. Leo thought the photographer could have sold it.'

'Och Rose, it's a wonder ye dinnae hae indigestion all the time from what yer gut churns up,' said Trixie.

Rose was about to retort when DCI Hickson arrived with Jones. Without a salutation she pointed at the back pack. 'Why didn't you have this sent straight to the police station or better still, tell me where I could find it, so it could be professionally handled?'

Rob and Trixie turned their heads back and forth in unison, observing the tense interaction between Rose and the DCI.

Rose took a deep breath, drew herself up and faced DCI Hickson head on. 'Firstly I didn't want you accusing me of wasting police time, if you check your phone you will see I did try to call you, before I called the airport. Secondly, I wore plastic gloves to handle the backpack and the contents, so I haven't compromised whatever you might find. It's already been handled by who knows how many people at the airport. You're welcome by the way.'

The DCI sniffed then gestured to Jones. He placed the backpack into a clear plastic bag along with the items of clothing and gift wrap.

'It's a pity you haven't learned more from Anthony. Working with the police and sharing information gets results as you'll soon find that out. Why were you at Torphichen Street earlier?'

'You were there? I didn't see you.'

'We're keeping an eye on you, Rose, and the house. All of the suspects are being monitored.' She turned and swept out of the door, with Jones scampering behind like an obedient hound.

'Talk about frosty, it's like a freezer in here after that performance.'

'Yeah,' Rose nodded. 'Our relationship does appear to have frozen over,' Rose looked up, open mouthed, as the bell on the door jingled and Kay walked in.

'All your relationships seem to,' said Kay. 'Perhaps try being nicer.'

'Kay! I...'

'I'm sorry, that was churlish. Rose, I've missed you very much.' Kay dropped her bags on the floor and, holding out both arms, waited for Rose to respond.

'I'll give you some space,' said Rob. 'Talk later.'

'Ah got tae finish that dough and other baking. Ah'll be in the kitchen.' Trixie said, and scurried into the back of the shop.

'Merry Christmas, or Happy New Year, or just hello.' Kay moved towards her.

Rose took a deep breath and accepted the hug. 'You changed your route home just to come and see me? How long are you here?'

'Two days, then I'm back on duty. I'm guessing you have your head full, trying to solve what happened to that girl whose hen party you were catering. The news she was murdered made it over the pond.'

Rose nodded. 'Yeah, but I've time for you too Kay. We need to talk.'

'I think that line tells me all I need to know. You've changed your mind about us?'

'I feel very confused to be honest. This murder had dragged up what happened to a man I had a brief affair with, I told you about Chris. Before he was murdered I'd suspected him of being a murderer. I just don't seem to... to be able to have normal relationships with people who love me without something happening to them. Like mum. If I hadn't fallen for Troy, she would still be alive.'

'Well, I'm not planning on being murdered and certainly have no reason to become one, even though you are very very annoying.' Kay smiled and held Rose's hand. 'I can't promise to wait forever, while you figure it out I mean; but I would like to stay friends.'

'Me too. I'll get my key. You can freshen up at mine. I can't leave Trixie to prepare everything for tomorrow on her own. But I won't be long.'

'You OK Rose?' Trixie said when Rose joined her in the kitchen. 'Was Kay arriving a guid surprise after the tongue lashing frae DCI Frosty or naw?'

'I don't know Trixie. I wish she'd called me before she changed her flight. She said that she knows my head's full, but I don't think she has any idea what that really means.'

Later, back at Rose's flat in Corstorphine, Kay watched while Rose pinned the newspaper cuttings onto the boards on the wall.

'That man, Hoffman. He's the one who murdered Chris?'

'Yes, and after Belinda the bride-to-be was murdered I learned that he was related to her. But I'm pretty sure he didn't have anything to do with her death.'

'Really?'

'There's a connection though, I just wish I could find it.'

'Why do you really do this? Get involved in police business I mean.'

'It seems to find me and I did try not to get involved, but...'

Kay looked down. 'I think you need to keep proving to yourself that you weren't responsible for your mother's death.'

'Are you psychoanalysing me?' Rose said remembering how she felt when she learned that Troy had been responsible for the fall which had killed her mother. The death had estranged Rose from her father for years.

'When I first met you, at your father's bedside, your face told me you were in a lot of pain. You cover it well, you're brave, you present a mask to the world. You even try to hide the molecular disease. Most people don't realise that you're almost blind or that that one good eye is failing much faster than you let on.'

'Yeah, yeah, I'm such a tough cookie.' Rose got up from the couch. 'I really can't talk about this now, I'm sorry. I've made up the bed for you.' She headed into the bathroom and closed the door. Kay's reminder of her physical and emotional shortcomings were overwhelming. She needed to escape. She'd just stepped out of the shower when she heard the front door close. The flat was empty. Kay had left a note on the coffee table.

*I'm hurting too, Rose. Two fragile people don't make for a healthy friendship, let alone a relationship. Goodbye and good luck with the new shop. I'll be in Edinburgh for a conference this month, maybe we can have coffee. Kay x*

Rose screwed up the note and threw it against the wall. 'Damn it.' She pulled on a pair of sweatpants, a jumper and her coat and headed for the nearest shop. Three hours later, the escape she'd sought had taken her back to the brink of a life she'd battled not to return to.

# Chapter Fourteen

'You're OK love,' a heavyset nurse reassured Rose, patting her gently on the shoulder, as Rose surfaced from the nightmare.

'Where am I?'

'Hospital. You've had a nasty fall.'

Rose struggled trying to sit up.

'Please try to stay still, the doctor will be along to see you now you're awake.'

'I can't feel my legs, what's happened.' Rose blinked trying to adjust her blurred vision to the surroundings. She was in a room with three other people, two of them were sleeping. Another was reading a book.

The nurse returned and surrounded the bed with curtains just before a short man wearing scrubs arrived. 'This is Doctor Gadass,' said the nurse.

The doctor, who in Rose's opinion didn't look old enough to be out of high school, didn't smile. 'You're lucky,' he said in a matter of fact manner, without empathy. 'You could have died before you were admitted. But if you hadn't been drunk, you might not have needed to be admitted at all.' His silver framed glasses slipped further down his nose as he lifted his eyebrows. His blue eyes were cold belying his attempt at a smile, to cover up judgement and convey humour

The nurse standing next to him grimaced.

'I have referred you for counselling and physiotherapy. You will be out of here within the week. Good morning.' Without another word or waiting for Rose to respond he disappeared through the hospital curtain.

The nurse adjusted Rose's bedcover. 'He's a good doctor, just a little sharp, you mustn't mind. Your friend Rob is here, would you like to see him?'

'Yes. But what's the matter with me? He didn't say.'

'You have some stitches in the side of your head and a trapped nerve in your lower back which needs rest, you should start to feel a bit better tomorrow, but walking is likely to be painful for a few weeks. The physio will help you with movement and exercises.'

Rose sighed deeply, she had no memory of anything after taking a shower and realising Kay had left.

Rob shuffled in, his face was grey and he looked tired. 'For goodness sake Rose, why didn't you call me?'

'I have no idea how I ended up here.'

'You went on a bender and decided to ride your e-bike. A passer-by found you and called an ambulance. They thought you were out cold from drinking, not falling off the bike. But it seems it was both.'

'When?'

'Two days ago.'

Rose groaned.

'It's all good. Trixie and I opened the shop as planned; today we closed early because we sold everything. Your banana curry muffins are a hit. The student you'd interviewed before Christmas is helping out, but we will need to find someone else, and probably delay the opening of the new shop.'

'I'm an idiot.'

'Yeah, that's what Anthony and Trixie said. But you're our idiot and we love you anyway.'

Rose smiled feebly.

'I've been to the flat. I'm sorry, I read Kay's note. I also cleaned up; you'd been sick. Do you remember tearing up the boards you made? You'd written this, it's a bit cryptic, but I guess you thought of something?'

He pulled out a piece of torn paper.

Rose shook her head. 'No idea. What time was I out on the bike?'

'After midnight.'

'As I said before, I'm an idiot.'

'Yes, indeed,' said Anthony, as he approached the bed, clutching a bouquet of white flowers. 'I don't know if hospitals allow flowers anymore, but...'

'Stop, both of you. I don't deserve...'

'No self-pity please, not on my watch,' said Rob.

'Nor mine,' said Anthony. 'Especially as I have some good news.' Rob and Rose waited expectantly for him to finish. He smiled at Rose and nodded. 'Hoffman has been arrested!'

'What! How?'

'There've been other arrests too, I don't know who exactly, but I would imagine that there's more than one senior ranking official in custody. Mind you, those names might never be revealed.'

'I can't believe it,' said Rose, her eyes tearing up.

'Was it anything to do with the house on Torphichen Street or the lab we found?'

'No. Seems that the work I'd done and handed in to DCI Hickson connected some dots after all, although I'm sorry to say Rose, his arrest isn't for murdering Chris.'

'So that's what she meant,' said Rose, remembering the DCI's comments in the shop about working with the police and sharing information being the way to get results. 'But, what about the higher ups, the ones who'd been protecting him?'

'According to the news this morning, we have a whistle-blower to thank.'

'You two are a force to be reckoned with when it comes to clearing up crime,' said Rob, patting Anthony on the shoulder.

'Or not so much. God, why did I tear up those boards? There was something I'd realised made sense, but it's gone.'

'Were the boards completely destroyed?' Anthony looked at Rob.

Rob shrugged and nodded. 'You don't want to even think about touching them.'

Rose groaned, 'Oh heavens to Betsy, don't even say it. I'm a disgusting drunk.'

Rob sat on the bed and closed his hand over Rose's, 'Never, that, and you've cleaned up worse from me remember.'

The nurse who had attended to Rose earlier came back through the curtains. 'Time for your vitals dear. Sorry boys but you'll need to give us a moment; and from the looks of this one, she could do with resting.'

Rose's eyes were already closed by the time the nurse had finished doing what she needed to do. When she fell back to sleep the nightmare that had woken her previously returned. She was on a carousel, the horse she was riding changed into a tiger. The animal raised its head back and roared, unseating her. She fell to the ground. The other riders who had joined her on the ride, Leo, Trixie, Rob, Belinda and Amanda slid off their mounts. They were no longer human, they were zombies. The carousel began to spin faster, the zombies walked towards her, until they had her in their grasp. The music became a cacophony of unharmonised howls and shrieks layered over the familiar organ music. The zombies dragged her from the floor and the carousel slowed down to a stop. The zombies lifted her above their heads and marched towards a big red circus tent. Inside, the tent was packed with hundreds of zombies seated in the grandstand and stalls. When the troupe dropped her onto the floor of the centre ring, the audience started to clap slowly. She looked up. The circus master, brandishing a whip, stared down at her. It was Chris. He swished the whip close to her and told her to get up. The audience stood too. Trixie and Rob stepped back into the ring and forced her to climb up onto a round podium. Chris swished the whip again; a rope ladder was lowered down onto the podium from the trapeze.

'Climb it,' demanded Chris.

The audience began to chant. 'Climb it, climb it.'

'Climb it Rose,' shouted Trixie and Rob as she turned to look down at them from the podium.

Chris cracked the whip again; Rose jumped and began to climb the ladder. She was almost at the top, reaching for the bar of the trapeze when her foot slipped. She called out as she fell, waking herself up.

The ward was low lit and none of the other patients appeared to have been disturbed. Each of them was breathing lightly and she could hear little snores from the woman opposite. Her body felt clammy, she was desperate to pee and drink water at the same time. She pushed the button the nurse had fastened to the side of the bed and waited. She loathed hospitals but she loathed feeling helpless even more. When the nurse had finished attending to her needs she thought about the dream, seeing her friends turn against her. Chris as the controlling and seemingly evil ringmaster when he had been the victim. The only thing that made sense was the fall. She had fallen when she'd given into the gremlins that haunted her; she'd let down her friends. They had turned against her, and who could blame them. She thought about Hoffman, she had thought that she would be celebrating with Anthony when he was finally arrested, but here she was in a hospital bed.

'What an unworthy loser,' she muttered.

She reached over for her phone and the notebook Rob had brought in for her and looked at the scrap of paper. A+S? What had she been thinking when she wrote that? Everything that had been on the boards would be in the notebook, except for the newspaper cuttings. She checked the texts and messages she'd missed. Amanda had called twice but not left a message. Apart from that everything else was to do with business and opening the new shop. She really didn't want to delay the opening. Trixie deserved her own place. Rose sent Amanda a text.

*I'm ok but out of action in the hospital. Can you visit me?*

Rose looked at the scrap of paper again and remembered. She hoped she was wrong.

The hospital was beginning to wake up, the shift changeover had begun. Rose watched a tall Asian man with a mop gracefully moving between the beds as if the handle of the tool was a dance partner. The same nurse from yesterday came to check on Rose.

'How are we?' She smiled broadly. 'No more nightmares I hope. You're looking a lot better than yesterday.'

'When can I get cleaned up, properly I mean, not...' she nodded towards the bowl of water and cloth that a younger nursing aid was carrying over to one of the other patients.

'Patience, my dear, and you'll be right as rain in no time. Doctor has said you can eat solids today, and we'll be raising you up in bed, trying to get you moving before you go home. Too much bed rest isn't good for your back.' Her unfaltering smile and benevolent tone was beginning to grate. 'Physio is coming to see you shortly,' she said, as if she were announcing a visit from royalty.

Rose clenched her teeth. She knew the woman was doing her best and she felt horrible being so judgy. After all, when were kindness, good humour and a smile not an attribute?

'I need to do a bit of tapping,' she said and waved a small implement in front of Rose, before she felt under the covers for Rose's legs. 'Ah, very good,' she said as Rose's left leg did an involuntary shake. 'And again, let's try the right.' Satisfied with the non-verbal response from her patient, she smoothed out the top covers and adjusted the bed so that Rose was in a semi-sitting position. 'OK?'

Rose nodded.

The nurse winked and gave her a menu card. 'Tick what you'd like although this morning you're too late to choose, so it'll be porridge.' She reached over and checked the stitches in Rose's scalp before she bustled away.

Rose gagged on the watery porridge and sent Trixie a text pleading for muffins. The raised sitting position made it easier to text and review her notebook. The introspective woes that had beset her earlier were diminishing and the disturbing dream no longer felt like a warning of ominous events yet to come. How wrong she was.

# Chapter Fifteen

Rose opened her eyes when she heard DCI Hickson's voice beyond the curtain. 'I'm awake,' she called out, her normally strong voice sounding thin.

The DCI and the nurse appeared at Rose's bedside. 'Are you sure you're up to talking to the police?' The nurse asked, looking concerned.

'Yes.' Rose looked over at the DCI, 'we know each other.'

The DCI pulled up a chair and sat leaned in close to the bed. She held up a mobile phone in a case, bearing the name of Amanda's yoga studio. 'Why did you send this text?'

'Why do you have Amanda's phone?'

'Amanda was run over this morning. She is dead.'

Rose felt her heart start to beat faster. 'What the... It wasn't an accident. You do know that right?'

'It was a hit and run, so whether it was an accident or not, we are looking for the driver. Why did you want to see Amanda?''

Rose opened her notebook and showed the DCI what she had written.

'I don't get it.'

'Amanda told me she thought that Belinda was already in bed and asleep when she came out of the bathroom. But she also said the reason they were sharing the bedroom the night before the wedding was to make a memory, they were two single sisters and one of them was about to be married. So why would Belinda have just gone to sleep without saying anything or calling out to Amanda? It was only when I re-read my notes this morning that I remembered. It seemed odd when she first told me I mean.'

'They'd been drinking, it makes you sleepy.'

'They had been drinking but everyone was still pretty lively when they went upstairs.'

'And that's what you wanted to talk to Amanda about?'

Rose flushed. 'No actually, well kind of. I made the same mistake I'd made before. I suspected the wrong person.'

The DCI frowned. 'Do you mean the Hoffman case? You had initially suspected one of the victims. Is that right?'

'Yeah.' Rose looked down, 'not one of my finer moments.'

DCI Hickson didn't respond and continued to praise the former policeman. 'Thanks to Anthony's thoroughness and persistence, Hoffman has been arrested and is facing serious criminal charges. So what was your theory this time?'

So much for the compliment the DCI had given her at the beginning of the investigation Rose thought, inviting her to contribute a map and any ideas she might have had. 'It was a vague hypothesis. I mean, I know her... knew her. I didn't want to believe Amanda was somehow involved in whoever killed Belinda, but it seemed like the only explanation.'

'Yet now she's dead. Who else is on your radar Rose?'

'Last time we met you made it clear you wanted me to stay out of it and, as you can see, I've now got myself into enough bother not to continue.'

'Despite which, when you thought Amanda might be an accomplice or even a murderer, you asked her to come and see you. If you weren't interested in following things up, why do that?'

Rose shrugged and held the steady gaze of the DCI. She could out stare anyone. The DCI looked away, adjusted her black jacket, then stood to leave. 'Do let me know if you remember anything else Rose.'

'Yeah, yeah I'll do that,' Rose muttered, trying not to rise to the sarcasm. She sent Rob a text.

*Would you have time to pop over to Thistle Street?*

She crossed out the earlier maps she'd made and began again. She printed the names, Belinda, Amanda, Leo, Mhairi, in a line across the top then she wrote Kyla, Sinead, Neive and Caroline below. In the middle of the paper she wrote Sally + ?On a new line at the bottom of the page she wrote Mark Monkton/Monkton Family/Sinead's Dad. Rose tapped her pen and thought about the newspaper article that had caught her attention.

'Ah hope ye approve o' these,' Trixie's voice was a welcome interruption to her thoughts as she handed Rose a bag with two muffins inside. 'Ah also brought you a latte frae the downstairs cafe tae go wi' them.'

Rose held up the bag to her face and inhaled. 'They smell delicious,' she said, savouring the mixture of pungent spices and banana. She broke the muffin in half and took a bite, allowing the soft dough to fall apart in her mouth. 'Mmm mm mm, well done Trixie.'

'It's your recipe, ah didn't change a thing. And, ah hope ye like the other one ah made.'

'Let me finish this bite and settle my taste buds.' Rose sipped on the coffee and then some water before trying the second muffin, flavoured with rose water and pistachio.

'No wonder you sold out of everything early yesterday, the flavour is perfect.'

'The customers really like them, the chocolate cream cheese an our familiar standard flavours are selling well tae.' Trixie sniffed at the congealed plate of lunch Rose had left. She wrinkled her nose and stuck out her tongue.

'Yeah, the food in hospitals means you *really* don't want to stay long. It was the main thing Caroline moaned about when she was in the hospital in London.'

'I brought over the post and the letter you wanted, from the solicitor about the new lease. 'Ah really understand if we can't go ahead now Rose.'

'Rubbish, of course we're going ahead. How's that student working out?'

'Braw, hardworking, punctual and does what he's asked.'

'Good, so assume it's all going to happen, as we planned for February 1st.'

'But ye cannae Rose, the injury ye'll nae be up for working full time for weeks. An' it's already January 6th.'

'The physio said a month, well I'll have to do it in three weeks, they're discharging me tomorrow. Rob will help and we already have three applications from the women's shelter. The same programme you came through. And look how that's worked out!'

'An look how much training ye had to gi' me. Naw Rose.' Trixie shook her head.

'My business, my decision and that's final,' Rose said, daring Trixie to argue.

Trixie was about to retort when Rose's phone pinged. It was Rob.

*Sally isn't in today. She drives a Silver ford focus. I asked the assistant; the shop was busy..*

*Her second name is Ferguson?*

*Yeah, Sally Ferguson.*

*Good. Is there a framed picture of this guy on the wall?* Rose attached a picture from the newspaper of the man who'd skipped bail.

*Yeah!*

*Where r u now?*

*I'm back outside the building.*

*Could you try to get in upstairs? To the publisher's office?*

*Why? What am I looking for?*

*IDK, but you'll know it if you find it.*

*?*

*A paper trail of some sort, connecting the name Ferguson to the publishers.*

*I'll try. I think I may hate you right now Rose.* His words were followed by a heart and a smiley face emoji.

'What's that all about?' Trixie asked.

'I've asked Rob to do a bit of breaking and entering,' Rose grinned.

Trixie got up, 'That's nae funny Rose. Wha's happened tae you? Yer nae thinkin' at all. Ye cannae keep puttin' him in harm's way. Sorry, ah need tae get back. If Rob's nae there I cannae leave the wee student by himself.'

'Wait, Trixie I'm sorry,' she called out. But Trixie had already gone. The colour drained from Rose's face as she remembered the dream and she sent Trixie a text.

*Sorry, followed by a sad faced emoji.*

She searched online for the name Sally Ferguson author. Three books appeared, two were on Amazon, the other was referenced in a blog post. *The Dirty Nurse* didn't appear on any second-hand book sites for sale. The cover image of a nurse bending over a female patient in bed was crass and amateur. The blogger had included the book as an example of fem erotica, but the review was poor and the writer didn't recommend it. She zoomed in on the image of the nurse. She thought about the images they had found on the USB stick she had shown to Leo. He had been upset by the photographs of Belinda spread tantalisingly over cushions and posed on a bed, had he known about this one?

She sent Rob another text.

*Can you find any paperwork for books WwW published before Leo and Belinda got together. Can you get onto the computer?*

*I was about to text you. The offices have been cleared out. The cabinets and shelves r empty. There r no computers or phones.*

Rose tapped her pen against the notebook, trying to make sense of all the different connections. Sally the hairdresser had been booked for the wedding, yet she'd deliberately chosen not to mention that. There was a photo in the hairdressers, the same man who was in the papers for skipping bail on charges of fraud and now Hoffman, the master fraudster, had been arrested thanks to a whistle-blower.

.oOo.

Rose was tired after the physio. She hadn't wanted any visitors, but she didn't have the heart to refuse Anthony when he popped in to check on her at the end of the day. He had been telling her about his evening with Cathy when Rose interrupted him.

'What did you give the DCI to trigger Hoffman's arrest?'

'OK Rose, what's bothering you?' Ever since I told you Hoffman had been arrested, you've not exactly celebrated. I thought you'd be happy.'

'I am, but the timing, it just seems odd and well convenient.'

'Convenient?'

'Yeah, something's not right.'

'You said Hoffman had nothing to do with Belinda's murder.'

'I'm not so sure now.'

'I give up. When I came down to London with you, on New Year's Eve, I put you before Cathy. She and I were supposed to have been at a ceilidh. I was going to meet her son and his family. Instead I chose to come to London with you. I'd already told you I was handing all my research on Hoffman to the DCI. Now he's been arrested. What exactly is the problem? Why is it you don't appreciate what other people do for you?'

Anthony put on his coat and reached out his hand towards Rose's shoulder. 'I'm going to go before I say something I might regret but think on. Whatever drove you to relapse, or to try and solve what happened to Belinda, those are your choices, don't blame the rest of us when things don't turn out the way you expect them to.'

Rose closed her eyes and turned her head away. She didn't want him to see the tears that had started to roll down each cheek. First Trixie and now Anthony, Rob was almost certain to be next. Trixie was right, she'd had no right to put him at risk, asking him to break into the WwW offices. Even Kay had told her to be nicer.

That night the nightmare returned, only this time Anthony was the ringmaster. Yet again she woke up with a start when felt herself falling, just as she was about to climb on to the trapeze. She looked out of the window of the small ward, everyone else was sleeping. Snow was falling again. The inky black sky lit up with white flakes reminded her of a story her mother had told her, when she was a child, about a boy who had become lost in the snow and was eventually rescued by an angel. She started to hum the tune of the only carol she could remember, *In the Deep Midwinter,* wishing for an angel.

# Chapter Sixteen

Rose strapped the support belt around her lower waist, pulled on the grey wool top and adjusted her leggings over the belt. Three weeks had passed since she'd left the hospital, and she'd made good on her promise to ensure the new shop in South Queensferry would open on time.

She checked herself in the mirror and sighed. She felt twenty years older than forty one, her complexion was flat and pale, walking was still painful. She touched up the bags under her eyes with concealer and applied light makeup to her cheeks and lips.

'There's a fair amount of traffic, hen,' the taxi driver announced as she manoeuvred herself into the back seat. 'It'll be faster if I go out via Kirkliston, ye a'reet wi' that?'

'Do your best, I don't mind,' said Rose as the taxi hiccoughed through the built up traffic in Corstorphine, taking the longer route to South Queensferry. The official opening for the shop was at noon. Trixie had told Rose she wanted to manage the occasion herself and Rose had obliged. The cooling between them as friends hurt and Rose didn't want to rock the boat in their professional relationship.

The colourful exterior paintwork on the buildings in South Queensferry reflected in the yellow winter sun as the taxi approached. Rose smiled when she saw Trixie's serious expression while she concentrated on finishing off the display of muffins and biscuits in the window. With Valentine's Day approaching she had been right to feature the old Forth Bridge and capitalise on the colour red. She had created a display of red velvet cupcakes, raspberry oat muffins, cranberry pecan muffins, heart shaped shortbread and lattice topped individual strawberry pies.

'It looks fabulous, well done,' said Rose.

'Oh, you're late, I was getting worried,' said Rob, through a mouthful of muffin.

'These are so good,' he said pointing to his mouth and then at a plate of baking.

'Nae more Rob!' Trixie replied sternly, wagging her finger. She turned back to setting out plated samples on the top of the counter ready for the queue of customers who were beginning to form outside.

Rose looked over at Trixie, but Trixie didn't look at her and carried on plating the samples. She stood awkwardly in the middle of the shop, waiting for Trixie to say something. Anything. 'What can I do to help?' Her words hung in the air.

Rob spoke quickly, filling the awkward silence. 'There's just the ribbon left to do, we waited until you arrived before we tied it in front of the door. Brand new scissors on that table.' He pointed.

Rose sat down on one of the tables by the wall. The decor complemented the shop on Morrison, they had kept to pastel colours but instead of pictures of Rose in the RAF, Trixie had embellished the walls with a mixture of funny, mindful and positive quotes from famous bakers and TV personalities who appeared on baking shows in the UK.

There were also photographs from newspaper cuttings and reviews about Muffins on Morrison, featuring Rose, Trixie and Rob.

Rose looked out of the window beyond the small crowd of customers, towards the Firth of Forth and the new Queensferry crossing. She felt conflicted. By pursuing what had happened to Belinda she had managed to alienate two of the three people she was closest to, since she had opened the shop.

She knew Anthony couldn't come to the opening because of the meeting with the procurator fiscal, to discuss the evidence he had built against Hoffman before he retired. The bigwigs who had protected Hoffman had all squealed, trying to save their own skins. Their last conversation about the meeting had been cool and uncomfortable.

'Should I fix this now...' Rob held up the red satin ribbon.

'Aye, the photographer from the paper said she'd be here a few minutes early. Rose, she'll probably want a photograph of you outside as well as inside.' Her voice was matter of fact, she could have been talking to a stranger.

Rose's face flushed. The frustration she had been trying to suppress rising to anger. 'Trixie, whatever has happened between you and I on the friendship front, don't forget this is still *my* business.'

'Come on you two. Please!' Rob exclaimed, as he closed the door behind him. 'The photographer's here, she's going to take pictures of the crowd, then Rose cutting the ribbon, then interior shots with the customers. This isn't the time for...' Rob spun and faced Rose. 'For goodness sake Rose. look what Trixie's done for you. What we've both done.'

Rose held up her hands and stood. 'It hasn't always been a one way street, or do neither of you wish to remember that?''

'Ah'm nae sure ah should be photographed after all.'

'Get over yourself, you too Rose. None of us is perfect. We've been through hell, individually and together. We're pals, it should take more than a few misspoken words to break us. Isn't that what this means, Trixie?' Rob pointed to one of the quotes she had stencilled onto the wall. *Life is what you bake of it!*

Trixie nodded. 'Well aye, but...'

'No buts Trixie,' said Rob and looked across at Rose. 'Well?'

Rose sighed, 'I hate this, not being... Oh, I don't know, friends, pals, whatever we are, you both mean the world to me. I'm sorry.' She opened her arms wide and invited the others in for a group hug.

Trixie nodded. 'Let's save the hug for later, or we'll all end up bawlin' like babes, and that wouldn't look guid in the photies.'

'Deal,' said Rose. She opened the door and stepped under the lintel, into the doorway, behind the ribbon. The crowd gave a small cheer when she cut the ribbon and announced, *Muffins on the Forth* was open.

.oOo.

When the last of the customers left, Rose, Trixie and Rob worked alongside each other to clean the shop, as if the unnavigable wall between Rose and Trixie had never existed. Chatting and laughing they finally collapsed around a table with fresh hot mugs of coffee. They had just

131

agreed to order pizza when Rose's phone pinged with a text from Anthony.

*Good news, looks like a Scottish trial will go ahead. International trials might follow. Hopefully Hoffman's finally done for.*

Rose took a breath, and then typed, *and Chris?*

*Afraid not. Not enough evidence. Theft and fraud.*

*So he'll get away with murder?*

*Looks that way.*

*No justice.*

*Sorry.*

'You ok?' Rob said, noticing Rose's face.

She passed him her phone and watched while he read the texts from Anthony.

'That sucks, but at least he'll be...'

'What? Sentenced for fraud and white collar crimes? He's a killer, you and I both know that.'

'Let's nae fall out again,' said Trixie. 'Ah tak it yer talkin' aboot Hoffman.'

Rob showed Trixie the texts.

'Nae more ye can dae an at least Anthony finally got someone tae listen.'

Rose bit her lip. 'Well I'm not going to let whoever killed Belinda and Amanda get away with it, it's been six weeks since I found Belinda's body. Mhairi, Leo and Amanda have all died since then. The police seem happy to write the other three off as a suicide and accidents. I don't believe it.' She watched Rob and Trixie look across the table at each other. 'I know you think I should let the police deal with it, well I'm sorry but I can't sit back while nothing happens.'

'What about what happened to you and Caroline in London, almost getting shot? Aren't they doing anything about that? And the swag you found in the house, gold ingots?'

'That's just it. The ingots, the shooting, the fire at Torphichen Street, Leo's so-called accident, the back pack at the airport, the publisher's office being stripped of its contents. The police aren't connecting the dots, everything is being dealt with as if they are separate incidents.' Rose took her notebook out of her bag. 'How about a pizza and you two help me figure out what I'm not seeing?'

'An if we dae that, will ye promise tae show it tae the ice queen?'

Rose laughed. 'Yes, I'll show DCI Hickson and try to persuade her to take it seriously.' Rose opened the notebook at the page of names she had written down in the hospital. 'Three weeks ago I had almost convinced myself that Amanda had something to do with Belinda's murder, then, after she was run over I concentrated on Sally, the hairdresser.' Rose turned the page and showed them the photographs of the book covers.

'Wait, that's Belinda, isnae it?' said Trixie pointing to the cover of Dirty Nurse.

'Yeah, we know Belinda posed for the photographer she went to Barcelona with, for book covers, and she had lied to Leo about it. But this shot, it's in a different class, not professionally done. Now I'm able to get around a bit more, I'm planning to find him.'

'Who?' Trixie and Rob said in unison.

'The person who took this picture. His name is Alex Ferguson, his sister is Sally Ferguson, the hairdresser. I am pretty sure Sally wrote these books. Amanda didn't have anything to do with Belinda's murder, but she knew something. She just didn't realise it.'

'So you think Sally killed Belinda and Amanda?'

Rose made a face, 'I don't see how she could have murdered Belinda, there is no way she was in the house that night.'

'And what's her motive?'

'Yeah, that's the missing piece, if I can figure out the *why* I could figure out the *how* and the *who*. So I go back to thinking about the locked house; who was inside the night Belinda was killed - Amanda, Sinead, Mhairi, Caroline, Neive and Kyla.' Rose tapped her finger against Sinead's name. 'She and Amanda had met the Monkton's, and knew Caroline from the visit to New York. Her father's friend owned the house and her father is a shareholder in the management company who rents out the property.'

'Wait, how do you know all that, about him being a shareholder I mean?' Rob asked.

'Companies House, it's a mine of information. The police arrested an employee and the manager for the document lab in the basement of Torphichen. The employee who skipped bail is Sally Ferguson's brother, the photographer Belinda posed for.'

'Have you told the DCI any of this theory?'

'Yeah, but she didn't seem interested in the connection. After all, Sally's brother wasn't at the house that night either.'

'So, Sinead?'

Rose shrugged. 'I don't think she could have managed it by herself, she's pretty small, it would need two of them to move Belinda. Belinda was posed on the deck next to the hot tub, but she wasn't killed there.'

'Then where?'

'In the garden house.'

'But Rose, you saw them going upstairs . Caroline went up before the London crowd left.'

'But I didn't actually see Belinda go up with them. I was finishing unloading the dishwasher in the kitchen.'

Trixie shuddered, 'Och that's a horrible thought. That one o' her so-called friends, nae, more than one, would hae had somethin' tae do wi her murder.'

'Or actually murdered her,' said Rob. 'If Rose is right and no-one else was in the house.'

Rose drew out another plan of the downstairs, including the toilet where she had found the hidden access to the basement and the front living room. The kitchen/dining room and exterior patio are all interconnected, the french doors had been open, and the patio had been heated. 'The only way Belinda could have ended up back in the garden without any of us seeing her is if she had remained outside, after they all started dancing on the lawn when the London guests were still there.'

'But she came in, I'm sure she did. That top was pretty distinctive.'

'Exactly. We saw what we were supposed to see. But can either of you actually remember talking to or seeing Belinda when everyone came back inside. There was a panic by the London crowd to find coats, because their taxi turned up early.'

'But ah...?' Trixie frowned, 'did we really imagine seeing her?'

'Does that mean that all of them were involved! All of them except Caroline,' said Rob.

'How do you figure that?'

135

'Well, because she went to bed first, and she was back in America when Amanda was murdered.'

'Dae ye think Mhairi committed suicide because of what they'd done?'

'I'm not ruling Caroline out yet, and I've no idea about Mhairi. Anthony said that the police usually knew if there was something fishy about a suicide and there's been no change in their thinking so far. But, she's still not buried.'

# Chapter Seventeen

Early the next morning Rose started a new board. After talking things through with Rob and Trixie, Rose decided to prioritise finding out why Belinda, Amanda, Mhairi and Leo were dead, rather than who was behind it. She'd learned her lesson about jumping to the wrong conclusions. If she went back to the locked house theory she potentially had six suspects, two of whom were dead. She called Rob to check everything was OK at the Morrison Street shop.

'Hey, how are you?'

'We've not burned the muffins you froze, and the extra batches Trixie made for here are on the way over in a taxi. Last night you promised if we helped you figure things out you'd talk to the DCI.'

'Yeah, I will, but right now what do I say? I have a theory, no proof. I'm pretty convinced that it was Sally who came to the Torphichen house and took away the backpack with Belinda's clothes in it the day I was there. I'm going to talk to her.'

'Just be careful.'

Rose made her way over to the hair salon on Thistle Street, but Sally still hadn't returned to work and the other stylists had no idea if, or even when, she might be returning, they were worried about getting paid. She knew going to Sally's flat was a risk, especially if Alex was hiding out there, but she might find out something from neighbours, more than she'd been able to glean from the stressed staff at the salon. Sally lived on the south side of the city, close to The Meadows. She walked back to Princess Street to catch a bus.

South Clerk Street was busy with cars and pedestrians scurrying to get themselves out of the rain. She tried Sally's buzzer and waited. Rose slipped through the restaurant on the ground floor of the building a few minutes later. There was a stone wall between the rear of the restaurant and the communal garden area for the flats above, with a wooden door for emergency access. Rose pulled the metal bolt across the door to open it. The gardens were overgrown and neglected. She looked up at the windows of the flats. No-one appeared to be looking out from where she was standing and the ground floor windows all had bars on them.

Rose counted the windows on the first floor and concluded Sally's flat was likely in the middle. There was no way she was going to be able to climb up the wall in her current physical condition. She went back inside the restaurant, ordered a coffee to go and loitered between the restaurant and the front entrance of the flats. She didn't have to wait long for one of the other residents to arrive. Rose placed her foot between the door and the step, just as the door was about to click shut, and paused until the resident went upstairs. Sally's flat door was even more secure than Leo's had been and without Anthony and his set of mysterious magical keys she knew entry was hopeless. She was just about to leave when she heard a familiar voice talking to someone as they came up the stairs towards her.

Rose ran up the steps to the next landing and leaned over. It was Kyla, she was on her phone. Rose waited while Kyla unlocked the door and, holding it open with her foot, lifted the two cabin sized suitcases she had been carrying. Rose ran down the stairs and held the door open.

Kyla stepped backwards and finished the phone call, her face drained of colour when she saw Rose. 'What the heck are you doing here?'

'I could ask you the same question, mind if I come in,' she said, pushing past Kyla. The flat was bright and airy, surprisingly spacious. The dark grey laminate flooring was contrasted by lighter neutral paintwork in shades of grey, pink and green. 'This doesn't exactly say hairdresser to me,' said Rose.

'What?'

'Where is she, and her brother?'

Kyla shrugged.

'What's in the suitcases? They look new.'

'What do you want, Rose?'

'I came here to talk to Sally, I'm looking for her brother, but you'll do,' Rose pulled herself upright. She was at least six inches taller than Kyla, but in her current state of health she knew Kyla could take her down if she tried.

'I have nothing to say and if you don't leave I'll call the police. That DCI woman will soon make your day if she turns up.'

'I doubt you'll do that Kyla, because you, Sinead and probably Neive are up to your necks in what happened to Belinda.'

139

'No!' Kyla stepped backwards and collapsed down onto one of the two sofas in the centre of the room, in front of the faux fireplace. Then, covering her face with her hands, she began to sob. 'You couldn't be more wrong,' she said through gulps of air.

Rose sat down on the sofa opposite. The glass coffee table between them, a fragile demarcation of their opposing positions. 'So tell me, what am I so wrong about? Which one of you changed into Belinda's clothes that night, pretended to be her. It couldn't have been Sinead, it was either you or Neive.'

Kyla swallowed and blew her nose. Her wet face shone like a beacon in the half light. 'It was Sally,' she whispered.

'Sally, but she wasn't…'

'She was downstairs. It was just a lark, a game. None of ever thought that Belinda would be in any danger.'

'You'll need to explain. What was the game?'

Kyla's left leg started to gyrate up and down as she pressed the ball of her foot into the floor. 'It was Mhairi's idea.'

'Oh, that's handy, considering she's dead. What was? For goodness sake spit it out.'

Kyla nodded, 'We didn't… well, Mhairi said… it would be better if you three, the caterers, didn't know about what we were up to. Mhairi had paid for Sally's brother to take photos of Belinda, a wedding present for Leo. But we didn't want Caroline to know about it – she seemed rather judgy and wouldn't have approved. Sally's brother isn't that good but we couldn't ask the professional guy Belinda had posed with before, he was out with Leo's party, Sally went into the garden to change into Belinda's clothes while we were dancing, we figured  you - wouldn't notice another guest

140

outside in the dark. No-one noticed Belinda was missing, Sally made sure she hung out with Mhairi until the others left. It was dark and then we all piled inside. We'd arranged for the taxi to come early, so it would be just the six of us in the house, Caroline had already gone upstairs. But that was the last time any of us saw Belinda.'

'It's a bit of a story. How did Sally get into the house?

Her brother, Alex works for Sinead's Dad or his friend, I'm not sure. She was able to get through from the basement.

Did Amanda know about the photographs?'

Kyla nodded.

'Why on earth didn't she, well any of you, tell the police then? Why lie about Belinda being in bed and then ask me to help find out what happened?'

'Because we were worried that it might make Belinda seem, oh I don't know, as if she wasn't worth bothering with. Amanda thought you'd still get to the truth about who killed Belinda; she didn't for one minute think you'd assume it was any of us. But then you seemed fixated on the idea and we all agreed it would be better not to say anything. But in the end, she'd decided it was better to tell you, and then, the next day, she was run over.'

'When did Sally leave the house that night?'

'While you were in the kitchen. She hid in the upstairs bathroom and changed. Caroline made a fuss about the bathroom being locked and had to use the one on the top floor. Sally slipped out and I locked the door behind her.

'So what happened to the clothes Sally had on when she met Belinda in the summerhouse?'

'Sally was wearing them when she came upstairs with the rest of us. She left them in the bathroom and then she left. I locked the door after her, .'

'And Alex, where was he?'

'Well, that's just it. Sally swore that he wasn't there. She showed us the text telling her he was delayed. He'd said to go ahead with the clothes swap and he'd get there as soon as he could. Sally's scared. She hasn't seen or heard from Alex since that night. She asked me to pack up some clothes and drop them off near the bus station in the left luggage store.'

'What is she scared about?'

Kyla shrugged. 'She thinks something has happened... to Alex. She said she'd pick up the bags later.'

'You're lying, she won't be able to pick them up if you drop them off, she'd need the claim ticket.'

'I'm just doing what she asked me to do. I don't know how...' Kyla covered her face again. 'This must be what hell is like. I feel trapped in a story that has no ending. A horrible, vivid dream.'

Rose thought back to the dream she'd had in the hospital. 'I know something about what that feels like,' she said. 'I don't know what to believe. You should have trusted me when you asked me to help.''

'Amanda said you were solid. Yes we should have trusted you.'

'I need to look through some of Sally's stuff. I'm looking for paperwork, connecting Sally to WwW Publishing. The offices were cleaned out and their computers have gone missing.'

'Go for it, I'll get the bags ready. She said to pack for a couple of weeks.'

While Kyla packed, Rose began her search, opening drawers and cupboards, however unlikely, that might contain paperwork.

'Ah you beauty,' Rose muttered as she prised open a locked cupboard in the bedroom. It was full of files, a laptop and several shoe boxes, with handwritten sticky labels advertising the contents. Rose scanned the first few files. Each one contained a different manuscript, page after page of badly written erotic tales describing encounters between men with men, women with women, and men with women. Finally Rose found what she had been looking for, a contract between Sally Ferguson and WwW Publishing. It was dated two years earlier and signed by Angus Thornberry.

'Kyla, do you have any idea who Angus Thornberry is?'

'Sinead's dad.'

'But I thought Sinead's second name was Frew?'

'That's her mum's name. Thornberry is her dad's. He's always in the papers, one of the reasons Sinead went off to Germany after her parents divorced. She said she hated having a notorious dad, who was famous for all the wrong reasons. So she changed her name to her mums.'

'What do you mean, *famous for all the wrong reasons*?'

'He's a lawyer who represents the bad guys. The ones who probably should be in jail.'

Rose checked her phone and clicked on the Companies House website again. There was no mention of Angus Thornberry as a director of WwW Publishing.

'What year did Amanda and Sinead go to New York, for their 21sts?'

'Technically it was the year after. They were both twenty-two when they went, so about three years ago. Why?'

'I'm not sure,' said Rose, recording the details in her notebook to think about later. She needed to speak to Caroline. 'Where's Sally planning to go?' Rose asked, watching Kyla zip up the second case.

'I don't know, but she's not asked for a passport. All she said is that she's trying to find out what's happened to Alex.'

'If he's heading for jail, why not skip the country?'

Kyla shrugged, 'He was going to get paid for the photoshoot with Belinda, it's weird he didn't show up. He was always short of money.'

'But you said he worked for Sinead's dad or his friend who rents the basement, and he's a photographer.'

'He bummed off Sally a lot. Whatever he did was usually on the dodgy side, even the photography stuff. Pornography mostly.'

'Was the photoshoot really Mhairi's idea or was it Sally's? If her brother needed money to get away?'

Kyla stared blankly. 'But why would Sally do that?'

'Let's go and find out. Can you manage both bags? I'm still healing from a fall off my bike.'

Rose called an Uber and waited outside the lock-up opposite the National Portrait Gallery, while Kyla deposited the bags.

'I'm supposed to text her when the bags are dropped off, but the message won't go through.' Kyla showed Rose her phone.

'The cafe in the gallery is open, we'll watch from the window, that way she won't see us waiting for her.' Rose pointed to a table under the portrait of Ian Rankin. 'Seems appropriate, maybe some Rebus rhetoric will help.' Rose stood next to the table, to make sure she could see the luggage location from the ground-floor window. But three hours later, as the cafe closed, there was still no sign of Sally.

'The texts are still not going through,' mumbled Kyla.

'Then we've no choice, we need to tell the police what really happened the night Belinda was murdered. Who were you talking to on the phone when I arrived?'

'Sinead.'

.oOo.

It was after 7pm before DCI Hickson was available, she agreed to meet them at the Morrison Street shop. Kyla called Sinead and Neive to join them and corroborate the events of the night of the hen party.

'All of you could be charged, you've withheld important evidence in a murder investigation.' The DCI's eyes flashed as she looked at the young women and then at Rose. 'Although all I now have is a different version of a story, pointing the finger at two other people who are both conveniently missing. And there's no evidence that either of them were even at the house that night.'

'What's going to happen now, to us I mean?' Neive's voice was shaky.

The DCI sighed and turned to Jones. 'We'll need separate statements from each of them, best you do that down at the station. I'll follow shortly and bring Rose in my car.'

DCI Hickson tapped her fingers against her tailored trousers while Jones and the three women left. She avoided eye contact with Rose until the shop was empty.

'I should lock the door, to prevent late night revellers trying to come in. Is that alright?'

The DCI nodded and sat down at the window table.

'Coffee, tea?'

'Sit. You and I need to talk about what you knew and when you knew it.'

Rose pulled her notebook from her bag and sat opposite the DCI. 'I usually date my notes. Here.'

DCI Hickson turned over the pages in the book, scrutinising the various drawings Rose had made of the house, the lists of names in different orders with arrows pointing up and down the paper, and maps with names in circles. Her finger tapped against the last entry Rose had made earlier. Angus Thornberry.

'His name turned up when I started looking into Hoffman.' The DCI bit her lower lip and stared out of the shop window. The wet pavements reflecting in the glass threw shadows across her face, she looked troubled. 'I'm being moved from the investigation.'

'What!'

'This is between you and I, Rose; Jones doesn't know either. If you hadn't called me tonight, we probably wouldn't have seen each other again.'

'Is this because of Hoffman?'

'I upset quite a few people when I insisted on an investigation into what Anthony had handed in. If I hadn't, the evidence would have been filed, but nothing would have happened. But when Angus Thornberry was linked to Hoffman as Lance Cooper, things changed. Hoffman was arrested and the people who had been protecting him turned against him, to save themselves.'

'So you're being moved off this investigation because you thought Sinead's dad was involved with Hoffman? 'Is that why you asked me to think about what I'd seen or heard right at the beginning? What about the house, the basement with all those fake documents, the ingots upstairs?'

'None of it's in his name. We've charged his friend, and guess what? Angus Thornberry gets to represent him. I've been keeping my eyes on Angus Thornberry for a long time, before I came to Edinburgh, he's one of the reasons I wanted the post. He's gotten away with too much.'

'Like Hoffman? He knows people on the inside?'

The DCI nodded. 'North and south of the border unfortunately.'

'You think he had something to do with the shooting, the fire at the lock-up in London? I thought that was all staged. It's like the empty backpack at Torphichen, and the ingots, almost as if I was meant to find them.'

'We should go down to the station, so you can make another statement about today, what Kyla told you. And, I can't tell you to do this but. . .'

'Got it. My lips are sealed.'

# Chapter Eighteen

'That was totally unethical, I can't believe she told you to do that.' Anthony's face was red, Rose had never heard him sound so angry. Even when they'd quarrelled before, he hadn't shouted, especially in public.

'She didn't, it was just inferred, for a good reason and, perhaps to protect me. She knows I'm not giving up on Belinda or Amanda. Here are the tickets for the two cases Kyla dropped off last night, please. We just need to know if they were picked up and what time.'

'We?'

Rose blinked and pulled a face. 'Aren't you going to help?'

It was the first time they'd met since the row at the hospital. Despite the texts they'd exchanged regarding Hoffman, Rose wanted to mend things between them, and she needed his help. 'I know I've messed up, and you feel…'

'Don't tell me how I feel Rose. Cathy and I are booked to go on a mini break to York tomorrow, I can't, well frankly I don't want to let her down. I'm sorry, but I can't help, not this time. Is that why you chose this place?'

Rose looked down and fiddled with the coffee cup. She looked over at the window where she had waited with Kyla the day before, next to Ian Rankin's portrait. 'Yes, sorry I,I didn't...'

'Think Rose. You didn't think, you just assumed.'

The cafe was full of elderly and middle-aged groups of visitors. She didn't want to fight with Anthony, his loud protestations about what she had left out of her statement had already drawn attention. She couldn't face another round of quizzical glances and whispered comments from the tables behind and opposite. It was time to give up. 'No bother,' she said, and picked up the baggage claim tickets from the table. 'Enjoy York, I'll see you when you get back. Please bring Cathy for dinner, I'd love to meet her.'

Anthony let out a sigh and held out his hand, palm up. 'Give me those. I'll do this, but that's it.'

Rose knew smiling at this point would be misread. She hadn't tried to coerce him and she didn't want to risk upsetting the delicate tendril back towards friendship he was offering. 'Thank you,' she whispered as she put her arm through his on their way out of the cafe and they crossed the road to the left baggage storage.

He was back within minutes, minus the cases. 'They've gone, according to their records they were picked up late last night.'

'Man or woman?'

'No idea, the attendant checked the signature but it was illegible.'

'I thought these places were supposed to be secure.'

'Not when you're dealing with people who are used to committing fraud. Maybe Sally knows someone who works here.'

Rose shrugged, 'So that's that. Trying to find Sally looks like it will be impossible, unless I...'

Anthony looked at Rose and put his hand on her shoulder. 'Whatever you're thinking, you know I'm going to say don't.'

'Yep.' Rose shuffled her feet and gave him a hug. 'Thanks for today. I've missed you. Have a great time in York.'

Rose watched Anthony as he turned the corner, walking away from the gallery towards St Andrews Square. Then she sent a text to Sinead.

*What time is your flight to Germany? Can we meet b4?*

She was already on the tram to Edinburgh airport when the news alert flashed up on her phone.

*Two dead following M8 midnight crash. A man and woman died at the scene after their silver Ford Focus spun out of control. The car overturned at the Airdrie intersection. "The car didn't slow down to make the turn," a witness who reported the crash to emergency services told our journalist. Police state speed and wet roads contributed to the fatal crash.*

Rose shut her eyes and mouthed an expletive she hadn't used since prison. She scrolled through her phone looking for more information, but the names of the deceased hadn't been released.

The airport was heaving with travellers heading off to winter snow and sun resorts, after the Christmas and Hogmanay celebrations. Sinead waved as Rose scanned the landside coffee shop looking for her. 'What's so urgent? I have a horrible hangover,' she pointed to an extra large takeaway cup and made a face.'

'Where did you get that?' Rose pointed to the green military-style backpack, similar to the one she had found in

Torphichen Street and the one which had contained Belinda's clothes.

'Dad. He sent me two last year for my birthday. They fit a whole load of stuff and means I don't have to check in luggage.'

'This is awkward, but, your dad, how much do you know about his business?'

'Lawyering? Not a lot except he's often in the paper with some pretty risky types. I was fifteen when his other business collapsed. That's when mum and I left.'

'What did he do? Publishing?'

'God no, nothing like that. Financial advice and investments.'

'Why did your mum leave?'

'We lost everything. The house, the holiday homes and Dad changed. He was angry all the time. It wasn't the money she minded; it was his behaviour.'

'And you changed your name?'

'Yeah, look I don't want to bad mouth him, but to be honest, I don't like him much anymore. He's my dad so I keep in touch, but I don't want to know about what he does. When they found that basement full of stuff at Torphichen, I felt horrible. It was my idea to ask Dad if he knew somewhere we could hold the hen party. Amanda was pulling her hair out trying to book something. Everything was full, Beli had left it quite late to plan, with it being Christmas and all.'

Rose pulled out her phone and showed Sinead the news item about the crash. 'Did you hear about this?'

Sinead shook her head. 'So, it's a crash, they happen.'

'Sinead you knew them. Well you knew Sally.'

Sinead's mouth flew open, she leaned in to look at the picture of the car. 'You think that's Sally's car?'

'Yeah, and I think it's the same car that killed Amanda.'

'Sally was involved in the hit and run? No, absolutely not.'

'It might have been Alex, but I'm sure Sally knew about it. That's why she was on the run too.'

'So why tell me, why not the police?'

Rose pursed her lips, she studied Sinead's face.

'What? Why are you looking at me like that?'

'Did your Dad ask you to drop off a backpack, like this one, here at the airport?'

'No.'

'Sinead, you looked away before you said that. I think you're lying.'

'You think everyone is lying, Kyla told me what you said to her yesterday. Who do you think you are! I need to get to the gate for my plane. Don't contact me again.'

.oOo.

Rose took the bus back to her flat in Corstorphine. She'd purchased another board for the wall, then, after checking her watch, she telephoned Caroline. There was little point in small talk and she decided to launch straight in with her question about who Caroline was dating.

But, as soon as she heard Rose's voice, Caroline hung up.

'Well that went well, not,' muttered Rose, as she heated up something from the freezer. She had just started to eat when the buzzer went and she heard Jones asking to come up.

'OK, come up,' she sighed.

152

'This is DCI...' but Jones didn't have the chance to finish.

A thin moustached man appeared at the top of the stairs behind Jones and started to speak and, in a strong Scottish brogue. He informed her they had a warrant to search her flat and she was required for questioning at the police station.

# Chapter Nineteen

The duty solicitor didn't inspire Rose with confidence. She knew she could have done a lot better than that for herself if she'd insisted on her own representation, but she hadn't really taken the man who'd replaced Hickson seriously. Now, any chances she might have had of leaving the police station that night had vanished. She was charged with Belinda's murder and would appear in court the following day.

The evidence the DCI presented was compelling to the uninitiated. She had found the body, she had returned to the scene of the murder on several occasions, she claimed to have seen someone leaving the house, found an empty backpack and some gold ingots. Why would anyone leave an empty backpack and how did she discover the ingots if she didn't know the house? And finally, Jones had reported finding Belinda's lost earring during the search at Rose's flat.

'But why on earth would I murder Belinda? What's my motive?'

The DCI pulled a photograph out of the folder on the desk in the interview room. It was a picture of Rose outside Muffins on Morrison, talking to Olifer Hoffman, alias Lance Cooper. 'Wait! That's not real. That never happened! It's like the earring, the gunshots in London, it's all been staged.'

'You might have got away with that last time, claiming you were framed. But twice in a lifetime, where fraud and document theft is involved? I don't think so.'

'You can see from the records, I was exonerated, not guilty. I received compensation for goodness sake.'

The DCI looked at Jones. 'You recorded concerns about Ms McLaren and DCI Hickson; do you have a question?'

Jones leaned forward and coughed. 'I do sir. The report is on your desk, should I...'

'No, we'll leave it tonight.'

'You think there was something going on between me and DCI Hickson? This is madness.'

'They do say that don't they. Although I think Einstein's original quote, about repeating the same behaviours and hoping for a different outcome, used the word insanity.'

'I need to make another call.'

'That's not possible tonight, you'll be entitled to make one in the morning before court.'

She'd tried Rob earlier and left a message; But that call had been before she'd been officially arrested and charged. She could only hope that Rob would let Trixie know and that he would come to the police station to find out what was happening. The less than reassuring presence of the duty counsel had promised to see her at court the next day.

She crawled into a foetal position on top of the bed in the police cell and wept. Every time she closed her eyes she was back in the red tent, falling backwards from the trapeze. Her foot stuck in the top of the ladder while she dangled precariously looking down at the crowd of zombies chanting, 'fall, fall, fail, fail, fall fall, fail, fail,' over and over. The chant grew louder followed by a cheer when her foot slipped out of the rope and she began her descent, tumbling through the air. She was about to hit the ground when her body jerked, and she woke from the dream. The sense of falling towards her own death felt all too real.

She rushed over to the toilet and threw up, she'd barely eaten and her guts hurt as she wrenched out the bile. 'No, this can't be happening again' she cried out. Leaning against the wall she clasped her arms around her upper body and began to rock from side to side. Time seemed to stand still, there were noises beyond the green door, people walking, remote voices, and finally metal on metal and a key turning in the lock.

A uniformed officer came in. 'Roll or porridge?'

The choice took her back in time, to time served in prison. Rose shook her head. 'Coffee, black. Can I make that phone call now?' But the uniformed officer didn't reply.

She'd just finished the coffee when another uniformed officer told her that her solicitor had arrived. 'You have half an hour before transport will take you to court,' he said as he closed the door to the interview room. The woman sitting at the table wasn't the duty counsel from the night before.

'My name's Habib Singh. We have to be quick; I've read through the charges and seen some of the evidence against you.'

'Did Rob contact you? Last night I couldn't...' Rose stumbled over her words.

'I've been appointed by Doctor Kay Sandeep, she's offering to cover legal costs, at least to see if we can get you bail. I've spoken to your friends Rob and Trixie and someone called Chatterton, Anthony? That was by phone though. You have some strong advocates, Rose. You're well respected, dare I say loved? Try not to worry.'

'Kay hired you?' Rose sighed, 'I have money, Kay doesn't need to pay, I can.' She looked up at the ceiling, blinking back the tears. Was she really respected, loved? She didn't deserve it; the dream was right.

'But the charge against me, the evidence, rubbish, the photograph, all of it. Why on earth would I murder Belinda?'

'Motive is our opportunity for defence and for bail. Are you willing to do whatever the court requires? It may mean giving in your passport, signing a declaration, staying within a confined area of town'

'Of course, anything. I can't be here. 'But I didn't think bail was possible for a murder charge.'

'It is in Scotland, whatever the charge, so long as we can convince the judge you aren't a flight risk or likely to harm anyone. I'm going to use concerns about your health, your visual impairment, the fact that you are a businesswoman in Edinburgh.'

'But the earring? Isn't that pretty damning?'

'Did you take the earring?'

'No, of course not. I've no idea how it came to be at my flat.'

There was a tap on the door. 'Time,' called a man's voice from the other side.

'I'll see you shortly. Let me do the talking, ok?'

Rose nodded and followed the uniformed officer out of the room.

.oOo.

157

'This is just the beginning, you're bailed, but you cannot get involved in trying to clear your name. That's going to be my job.' Habib Singh took off her glasses to stare directly at Rose across the modern desk. Her fourth floor office in Leith was sparsely furnished, with black and white Scandinavian style furniture. The office walls were painted white with no ornamentation, apart from two framed certificates and a potted fern hanging in a macrame basket. One wall was lined with books.

'She's reet Rose, ye cannae,' Trixie chimed in. 'We're all here for ye, but listen tae wha' ye're being telt this time.'

Trixie, Rob and Anthony were sitting by the window, behind Rose. The three-seater sofa was barely large enough, but their closeness to each other was comforting.

Rose wished she could have squished onto it with them. She knew she needed to be very grown up, something she had thought she was good at before now.

'I have a theory, and that's what we need to prove, to clear me.'

'I can help you do that. But right now, your theory is all over the place. Before you were arrested you texted Rob to say that you knew the people you were looking for - Sally and Alex - had been killed in a car crash, and that Sinead's family were responsible for the murders.'

'So wasn't it them in the crash?'

'Nay, it wasnae.' Trixie's voice was quiet and she gave Rose a sympathetic half smile. 'Yer thinking isnae clear reet now. Yer heed is all o'er the place.'

It was Rob's turn to convince Rose she should stop. 'The car you read about *was* a silver Ford Focus, but the people who died were a married couple on their way home.'

'Oh my days, I'm sorry.' Rose put her head in her hands. 'But that photograph, the police have of me with Hoffman, that's a fake, and I didn't have the earring. How can I prove that?'

'By trusting me to do my job,' said Habib.

'But that doesn't mean you can't think, use your smarts to map things out. Just try to stop going off on tangents, making assumptions about things that lead you down rabbit holes.'

Anthony walked over to Rose and put his hand on her shoulders. He nodded reassuringly, 'We all know that photograph is a fake, like the earring, we need evidence to prove you didn't take it.'

Rose nodded. 'Maps at mine then. Thank you.' She looked back at Habib, 'How long until this is all over?'

The solicitor opened her hands, 'It's not going to be quick, although the police would like it settled and off their books. Send me all the names and numbers of contacts you have and how I get hold of Caroline Monkton. She's back in the States is that right?'

'Yeah, unfortunately.'

'That may be to our advantage.'

'How? And, just one thing more. How did Kay, Doctor Sandeep, know I needed a solicitor?'

'She's in Edinburgh, for a conference. When she couldn't get hold of you she called me. It was late by the time I listened to your message,' said Rob.

'Ah, the conference. She'd said she wanted to meet for coffee when she came up. I didn't think she meant it. I didn't expect to ever hear from her again.'

'Ha, ye hae a way of stickin' tae people Rose, even when ye tak the juice an behave lik a numpty.'

With Trixie's words ringing in her ears Rose sat silently in Anthony's car during the drive back to her flat. Rob and Trixie had gone their separate ways to try and salvage what they could of the day and get the two shops ready for opening the following day. Anthony followed her upstairs, they both gasped at the mess the police had left.

'You should report it, this isn't procedure.'

'Yeah, right, as if. A messy flat's the last of my problems, don't you think? Sorry, I didn't mean to snap. Trixie's right, I'm a numpty. I don't treat people the way I should and I don't listen.'

'Back to self-pity?'

'Ouch, that's a bit unfair.'

'Brutal maybe, but if you go down that road, I think you know the danger, don't you?'

Rose nodded. 'I'll make coffee, then clean up, I won't repeat what happened and drown my sorrows. There's a meeting later, Rob said he'd come.'

'I'll make the coffee, you shower and then we'll clean up together. Maybe we could make a map?'

'Really? Did I ruin York... I'm sorry if...'

'No, York was wonderful and yes, a day shorter than planned, but Cathy understood. She's pretty special.'

'You deserve special, and I'll make it up to you, to both of you. I promise.'

.oOo.

Rose clenched her jaw as the cold water hit her body, she'd started taking cold showers the day she left the hospital. She didn't like the sensation but afterwards she felt refreshed, more awake than after a luxurious bubble bath or the scalding hot showers she'd previously enjoyed.

160

She pulled on clean black leggings, a cream top and towel dried her short hair. By the time she re-joined Anthony the living room was tidy and the clean board she had bought to write up her theory lay on the dining table, along with her notebook and a selection of pens.

'You work fast,' Rose said as she made her way to the dining table. 'What are these?' She pointed to a pile of photocopied news articles.

'Your printer needs more ink; sorry I find it easier to handle paper than stare at a screen.'

'Me too, hence the notebook and the maps. These are articles about Angus Thornberry and the Monkton family?'

'I'm not so sure that you're completely off track about Angus. But murder, hmm that's not his MO.'

'Or it hasn't been to date you mean.'

'What's the motive?'

'The usual avarice, greed and revenge, for the fortune he lost. 'It's easier if I show you what I think. 'Rose sketched out a map in her notebook. She wrote out the names of everyone who'd been at the hen party, then added Hoffman and Angus Thornberry. She connected the names by a series of arrows flowing from Hoffman up to Angus on the one side and from the four women on the other. It looked like a weather chart with a storm culminating underneath Angus and Caroline. She then drew downward arrows from the storm towards the three names in the middle of the page, Belinda, Amanda and Leo.

Anthony sat back, holding up the notebook. 'Why is there a question mark under Hoffman?' He asked.

Rose shrugged. 'Alex and Sally, or someone in the police. Jones, the one who reportedly found the missing earring here?

'And Mhairi, why is her name with the other three women and not with Belinda, Amanda and Leo? She's dead.'

'I'm coming round to thinking that Mhairi was involved. I don't believe that they just left Belinda on her own in the summerhouse waiting for Alex. In fact I find the whole story about sexy photographs for Leo unbelievable now.'

'I agree, but we're back to motive. Why would one of her friends murder her and, if you're right, Leo and Amanda as well? May I?' Anthony fetched two clean sheets of paper from the printer and re-drew Rose's theory, separating Angus Thornberry and Hoffman from the other names and placing Sally and Alex on both sheets of paper.'

'I don't get it,' said Rose.

'Everything that's happened seems to also have a connection with these two. Sally was the hairdresser for the wedding party and claims to have been a friend of Mhairi. Alex is a photographer with a connection to Angus Thornberry. Have a read of those print-outs and I think you'll see what I mean.'

Rose had just finished reading the print outs when her buzzer sounded. 'Could be Rob,' she said, making her way to the door. It turned out to be Kay.

'I have food and humble apologies, if I'm allowed in,' Kay hovered at the entrance to the flat.

'Of course you're allowed in. That smells delicious,' Rose said pointing to the two white bags Kay was clutching.

'Rob's following on with dessert, consider this an intervention by invasion.'

'Oh, an intervention, lovely.' She said, unsure whether to laugh or cry. She needed a meeting more than anything but she didn't want to upset everyone again by appearing ungrateful. Anthony had been the epitome of saintliness all afternoon, when she suggested he take a break, he'd refused.

The penny dropped. 'So I'm being baby sat?'

'Aye Rose, ye are, ye'd better get used tae it,' said Trixie, brushing past Kay with two full grocery bags.

'Sorry Rose, I was out voted,' said Rob.

Rose shook her head watching her uninvited guests start unpacking food and setting up the table for dinner. 'This is worse than my nightmare,' she muttered and went into the bedroom. Sitting on the bed she stared at her reflection in the mirror on her dresser. 'I'm not completely useless,' she told herself. She hadn't seen Kay standing in the doorway.

'No, you're not useless,' said Kay. 'This probably feels overwhelming, but we all just want you to be safe.'

'Can you give me a few minutes? I needed to go to a meeting. Not host a dinner party.'

'This isn't a party Rose, this is your friend family, trying to support you. Why don't you get that?'

Rose walked back over towards the dresser, to the photograph of her mother. 'I do, I'm just not... I'll be out in a minute. Thank you.'

Kay slipped silently from the room; Rose sat on the bed staring at the photograph of her mother. 'I miss you so much,' she said. Then, wiping her eyes, she returned to join her friend family in the living room.

# Chapter Twenty

Rose sank into the cushions of her couch, savouring the strong coffee. She mouthed a thank you to the unspecified spiritual deity she reached out to in times of crisis, that she wasn't in the same place she'd been twenty four hours earlier. Her mother had attended church, her father was agnostic. Thanks to the twelve step programme, which she had first encountered in prison, Rose believed in a higher power, but she hadn't been drawn to or adopted a particular doctrine or theology. She'd slept well considering her life was falling apart and silently said another thank you for her tribe of friends. Trixie, Kay and Rob had insisted on cleaning up before they left. Anthony had left earlier to meet Cathy and said he'd call sometime in the morning.

She studied her bail conditions, she wasn't allowed to leave the UK or have contact with any of the women from the hen party, directly or indirectly. She emailed Habib with the contact information she'd asked for and reviewed the maps she and Anthony had done the day before.

Anthony's print outs confirmed that Angus Thornberry had lost everything, including his family. The paper trail about which investments were owned by who and why they went belly up was less clear, but given Hoffman was involved Rose wasn't surprised. Hoffman's skill was the ability to magic something from nothing and back to nothing again. Yet within a short time Thornberry's fortunes had changed yet again. His lawyering practice was incorporated and his firm had grown exponentially. There were offices in Edinburgh, London and New York. They dealt with property, criminal law and financial investments. Nothing to do with publishing, press or entertainment. 'So why would you get involved in a tiny publishing company?' Rose muttered.

Her phone pinged with a text from Anthony.

*Fancy brunch with me and Cathy? She'd like to meet you.*

*Thanks, but I don't think I'm my best self. Enjoy. X*

She leaned her head back against the back of the sofa and considered her plan.

When she'd been in prison, the chaplain had been the only one able to organise calls outwith normal limitations and take messages from family members to a prisoner. The practice was reserved for important family matters but, when she'd been inside, her ex Troy had lied well enough to manage to get her to the phone. Could she beat Hoffman at his own game? It was Saturday, the chances were slim, but she had to try. If what she'd figured out yesterday was right, Hoffman would agree to a visit from Sally. She didn't dare risk requesting him to see her under her own name in case the fact she was on bail was flagged.

Rose studied her hair in the mirror, she, and Sally both had short hair, although Sally's was a pixie cut, and there was a height difference, if she could get ID, she was certain she could pass gate security. Rose called a locksmith and made her way over to Sally's flat.

'So stupid of me to leave my keys with a friend, thanks so much. Cash OK?'

'Happens more than you'd think hen, aye, cash is fine. Need a receipt?'

Rose winked, 'No you're fine, here, have a drink on me later,' she told him and handed him a ten pound note.

Rose put the snib on the door and searched the flat for the second time. Sally had clearly not been back since Kyla had packed the cases. Rose tried the desk, the bookcases and all the cupboards she had looked through the last time. Eventually she found what she was looking for.

'Voilà,' said Rose, when she saw the passports. There were four of them, hidden in the linen cupboard under a pile of towels in a ziplock bag. Two of the documents had the correct legal names, but the other two had different names. Despite the long wig, Rose still recognised Sally.

Rose photographed the passports and the contract for the book with Angus Thornberry's signature. She doubted Habib would be able to use any of it in court, but at least she could show her proof of what she'd found. Then, using Sally's landline, she called the prison where Hoffman was on remand and asked to speak to the chaplain.

'I'll see what I can do. You're the prisoner's niece, Sally Ferguson, did you say?'

'Yes, I've just found out my uncle is in prison. Sorry my mum's funeral is on Tuesday, I'd like to see him before that, if it's possible.'

'What's the number, I'll call you back. I'll also need an address for the visiting order, even though it will remain here at the prison. Without an address, it won't be issued. You'll need ID and proof of your address too.'

'Yes, that's no problem. Thank you so much.' Rose perched on the edge of the chair waiting for the return phone call. She jumped as the handset rang, lifting the receiver she listened first, in case it wasn't the chaplain.

'Ms Ferguson, are you there?'

'Hello, yes sorry, it's me.'

'It's not going to be possible for you to come today, but there is space tomorrow for remand prisoners and your uncle has agreed to sign a visiting order. Can you be here for 2pm? The visits begin at 2.45 and finish at 3.30, but it takes a while for all the security checks and they won't let you in if you're late. I'm on myself, I can meet you if you like, or want support before or after you speak with your uncle. I didn't tell him why you were coming. He seemed surprised you wanted to come, but he certainly seemed pleased that you wanted to visit him.'

Rose grimaced as she continued the deception; she hoped there wasn't a hell or she would be condemned for sure.' Thank you, you've been very kind. I'll be ok.'

'I'll pray for you, and your family. The death of one's mother is never easy. I'm glad I could help.'

Rose put Sally's passport in her bag and rummaged in the desk for an official letter that would prove her address to the prison. The file of bank statements for the hairdressing business evidenced the salon had been in trouble until six months ago. Then a monthly deposit for just over nine thousand pounds had removed the overdraft and currently left Sally with a healthy balance of just over fifty thousand pounds. The most recent transaction showed a withdrawal two days earlier of five thousand pounds. Rose photographed the bank statements. Then she looked up the company who'd deposited the money, but there was no trace of the name at Companies House or via Google. She checked her phone and ordered an Uber, she still hadn't recovered enough to be actively on her feet for long. When she closed the desk she noticed a stack of business cards with the same logo as the torn one she'd found in the garden room at Torphichen Street. The name on the card, LJH Consulting, was the same company who'd made the deposits to Sally's bank.

.oOo.

According to the business card the offices for LJH Investments was close to the High Court of Session in Old Town. The area was full of shoppers and tourists making the most of the clear sky and winter sunshine, Edinburgh was at her best. The pavement cafes were full and a street performer on Grassmarket, where she used to have a mobile shop, was drawing a substantial crowd.

Rose made her way up Victoria Street and past St Giles Cathedral. She turned onto Market Street, but her journey ended in disappointment. The offices turned out to be a mailbox and printing business centre. She went inside, but she knew before she even opened her mouth that identifying the person who rented the mailbox, or came to collect its contents, would be hopeless. 'Well done, another rabbit hole,' she muttered as the woman behind the counter shrugged and shook her head.

'Rose?'

She turned around, it was Anthony. 'Oh my days, is this Cathy?' Rose smiled at the comfortably built brunette with her arm through Anthony's.

'It's guid tae meet ye Rose.'

'I thought you weren't up for going out?' Anthony looked her directly in the eyes. His unwavering stare caught her, she knew she wouldn't get away with lying.

'If you two aren't in a rush could I buy you a coffee, I'm assuming you've already had brunch?'

'Aye, we have, but a coffee would be grand,' said Cathy giving Anthony a gentle squeeze with her arm.

Rose waited until the coffee arrived before she told Anthony her plan. 'I know you'll try and talk me out of it, but it's done now. I have to see him. Habib is a good solicitor, but honestly, I don't think she has any idea of the depth of deception Hoffman and his police contacts will sink to and make this charge stick to me. Look how quickly they moved Hickson on after Hoffman was arrested. The photograph of me and Hoffman... I can't just sit and do nothing.'

'And your plan could make things worse. Rose, if you're caught, you will go to prison, on remand until the trial.'

'I won't get caught.'

'How do you know Hoffman won't out you, there and then?'

'I'm nae sure I understand wha's goin' on, but mebee listen tae Anthony? Ye're laik a daughter tae him, ye know that?' Cathy's warm green eyes held Rose in hers, her hand stretched across the table in a gesture of friendship.

'I shouldn't have told you. I realise I've put you in a horrible position, but I couldn't lie. Will you give me away?'

'No, I'm not a policeman anymore and you're right about Hickson. Whatever happened there doesn't sit right, One condition though.'

'What?'

'I drive you to Barlinnie tomorrow. If it goes belly up at least I'll be there to let Habib know you need her help urgently.'

.oOo.

Barlinnie Prison, referred to as *"The Big Hoose*, is situated on the north east of Glasgow in the suburb of Riddrie. The original building opened in 1882, and currently held about sixteen hundred men, sentenced or are waiting for trial. Rose shuddered as Anthony's car entered the car park. Her experience as a prisoner at Cornton Vale was relived briefly as she watched a steady stream of visitors make their way to the entrance.

Anthony turned to face her. 'You sure about this?'

Rose shook her head, 'Not really, but I think it's the only way to prove that photograph is a fake.'

'If you're right and he agrees to help you, you might be giving him a free ticket out of here. How does that give Chris justice?'

'I know, it's like I'm trading justice for one dead person against justice for three.'

'Hoffman has more than the blood of one human being on his hands.'

Rose opened the door slowly and climbed out of the car. Her lower back and legs hurt a lot, she'd tried to dismiss the pain as psychological, every step towards the entrance felt like a nail being driven into her. 'Another nail in your own coffin Rose,' she said under her breath, as she handed Sally's passport and the letter to the guard; she crossed her fingers, hoping he wouldn't notice the discrepancy in height. He studied her face before he looked down at the passport, then repeated the action several times. She breathed deeply and felt herself flushing while he examined her. She was just about to accept she'd failed when he handed her back the passport, stamped a sheet of paper and nodded at her to follow the queue of visitors who were lined up at the side of the desk.

Rose had just sat down at the wooden table in the visiting room when Hoffman appeared. His snort as he joined her made her want to heave.

'I was wondering who my niece Sally Ferguson really was. Well Rose McLaren, you're a treat for sore eyes. Or is that a bit of a painful subject?'

Rose straightened her back and clenched her jaw. 'Why didn't you think it would be Sally?'

Hoffman chortled, and let out a whistle. 'You're a cool woman, I have to give you that. Why would this Sally Ferguson come and visit me of all people?'

'Because she worked for you, you paid her and paid her well.'

'Nope, not me. You're off track there Rose.'

'What?'

'This is about my niece right? My real niece, Belinda?'

Rose nodded. 'And Amanda, she's dead too, a hit and run. I'm sure that wasn't an accident.'

'So? I didn't have anything to do with it. Is that why you came to talk to me?'

'I know, but I need your help. It might reduce your sentence if you help me.'

'Ha, that's a good one. What could you possibly do to make that happen? I would have thought you of all people were glad I was here. By the way I would have gladly given you a visiting order. Why the subterfuge?'

'I've been charged with murdering Belinda. There's a picture. It's fake, of us together. I need you to say it's a fake. I won't testify against you, if you agree.'

Hoffman opened his mouth, but no words came out. He leaned in closer, as close as he dared without drawing attention from a prison officer. 'You really thought that if you asked I would help you, is that right Rosy?'

'I hoped we could help each other. Did you have anything to do with me being arrested?'

'Oh that's a good un, If I had something to do with you being arrested, you wouldn't be sitting here now. Help you? I don't think so.'

'For your nieces?'

'I hadn't seen the girls for years, there was some trouble about their mother's trust fund and I was blamed. Fair do's, not my fault if the legal buggers didn't do their job properly is it?'

'Don't you care why they were murdered, or who really did it?'

'Not really Rose, I don't get attached, you should know that.'

'But you're not here because of what you did to Chris, your half-brother? You're here because.' Rose took a breath, she could feel her voice rising, the pitch was close to hysteria.'

'Woah, so you loved him, did you? My half-brother, fancy that.'

Rose wiped her eyes with her sleeve. 'You bastard,' she whispered and stood up. 'I shouldn't have come, I thought, I hoped you had a conscience of some sort. I was wrong.'

'Toodle pip Rose. Thanks for dropping by,' Hoffman wangled his fingers at her and nodded to the prison officer opposite.

Rose held her breath, was he going to give her away? But Hoffman merely winked as he left the visiting room with the guard.

'This way Miss,' another officer pointed to the door which said Exit.

Rose made her way through the busy visitors' room, out of the building and back to the car, holding the tears in for as long as she could, until they exploded all over Anthony. 'He's a complete bastard,' she sobbed.

Anthony stroked her head and pulled her in close. 'I know Rose, I know.'

# Chapter Twenty One

Rose stared at the blank sheet of board she had bought the day she'd been arrested. Her mind still felt scrambled after the visit to Hoffman, compromising her ability to make sense of what she knew, or what she thought she knew. She'd been wrong so many times about Belinda's murder. Hoffman hadn't seemed surprised when she'd told him she had been charged. He'd denied Sally was working for him, yet he clearly knew who she was; so was it possible he also knew Alex, and had employed him at some point?

'Come on Rose, think,' she said aloud, getting up from the table to make another pot of coffee. It wasn't quite dawn, and she hadn't been able to sleep after Anthony left.

She'd just settled down to try and start a new list and clear her muddled mind when her phone pinged with a text from Kyla.

*Can you call Sally. This is a landline number to the hotel in France.*

*What's happened? It's 5am! Can't you sleep either?*

*Nope. IDK why. Sally found Alex. Said she needs to talk. On it.*

Rose tapped in the number, put her phone on speaker, and opened the record call app while she waited for the receptionist to transfer the call. .

'Rose?'

'Hi Sally, Just so you know, I am recording this call. Kyla said you want to talk to me. What's this about?'

'It's Rose, she's recording the call.' There was a brief silence. Rose could hear a man's voice mumbling in the background.

'What is it Sally?' Do you know something that could help find out who murdered Belinda?'

'Sinead told me you'd been arrested.'

'How did Sinead know I'd been arrested?'

Rose waited while Sally deferred to Alex, discussing what could or should be said while Rose was recording the call. Then Alex started shouting. 'Say nothing.'

Rose hesitated. If Sally hung up or wouldn't speak she might never know what the call was about. 'Hold on.' Rose clicked stop recording on the app. 'OK I've stopped the recording, will that help?'

'Yeah. I'm sorry about what Alex... what we did, it's made things worse. For you.'

'You're talking in riddles. What did you do and again, how did Sinead know I'd been arrested?'

Alex grabbed the receiver, 'For god's sake Rose just listen will you. Sinead's Dad was furious when he found out that you were the one who'd broken into the basement, he told her that he'd make sure the police knew it was you who murdered Belinda.

'What! Sinead's dad was responsible for Belinda's death and then he set *me* up for it? I thought Hoffman, Belinda's uncle, had done that.'

'Sinead's dad set you up but he didn't kill Belinda. Caroline did.'

Rose, who had been pacing her living room during the call, collapsed onto the sofa. 'But that's impossible.'

'You can thank Sally's conscience I'm telling you. She thought you should know the truth.'

Rose shook her head. 'The truth? I wish I had ten pounds for every time someone claimed they were telling the truth since Belinda died. I thought you two had died in a car crash after Amanda died. If you knew about Caroline from the beginning, why didn't you tell the police.'

'How could I? I agreed to take the fall for a job which had gone wrong, Sinead's dad promised me he'd take care of Sally. Her business wasn't going well and he said that he'd help her keep the salon. But when it came to it, I couldn't do a long stretch. I would have gone down for ten years, so I ran. Trouble was Angus had already paid money to Sally.

'Was that why you created that photograph of me with Hoffman?'

'No, that was done a while ago, just after Hoffman's brother was killed. It was easy money and I didn't ask questions. Then he said he wouldn't need it after all.

'Why did he change his mind?'

'I don't know. He said he needed it after Sinead came back from New York. She'd got into some trouble, took some drugs and stolen money from the Monktons' house. The older son Mark and Caroline dealt with it. Angus was furious, but not with Sinead, with Hoffman. Hoffman was at the same party under the name Lance Cooper. Then Angus and Caroline became an item. I got the impression that Sinead wasn't happy about it.

'I knew about the affair. Caroline denied it when I called and asked her. But what makes you think she murdered Belinda?'

'I saw her do it, and so did Mhairi.'

'Jings! You have to tell the police!'

'I'm sorry, I can't. I can't go back to prison for something I didn't do.'

'But you think it's ok for me to go to prison? There has to be a...,' but the call disconnected. Rose pressed her keypad to reconnect.

'Pardon Madame, pas de réponse. Merci, au revoir.'

Rose sent a text to Anthony and then called her solicitor Habib. But neither of them responded. It was still early, not even six am. She dialled the hotel again and asked for the location. 'Oui, St Malo, voulez-vous une réservation?'

'Non, merci,' said Rose. From St Malo Sally and Alex could pretty much travel anywhere they wanted. From France they could cross different borders into other parts of Europe. Clearly they were travelling on false passports and under different names. 'Parlez vous anglais'?

'Oui, how can I help?'

'The couple I spoke to earlier, in room 24, are they still at the hotel?'

'Non.'

'Can you tell me what name they registered with, they just married, I...'

'Non, pardon, I cannot say this. Au revoir.' The receptionist disconnected.

Rose texted Kyla. *U still awake?*

*Yeah. How was Sally?*

Ignoring her bail conditions, not to have contact with anyone from the hen party, Rose invited Kyla over to the shop for breakfast.

.oOo.

Rose had just put in a tray of muffins from the freezer and brewed a pot of coffee when Kyla knocked on the door. 'You're early.'

'Yeah, it's not far to walk and I needed to get out. So, Sally?'

Rose poured them both coffee and sat opposite Kyla at the window table. 'If this table could talk,' she said.

'It's seen action eh?'

It's certainly heard its fair share. When I was newly open a girl was murdered outside, she worked for me at one time. This was the table that the police used to interview me about her.'

'You ok?'

'Not really, but hey you didn't come here to listen to me.'

'Well I kinda did.'

'Ah, well it's a story, I'm just not sure if it's true.' Rose told Kyla what Alex had said.

'He told you he saw her, and he saw Mhairi?

Rose nodded. 'How close are you to Sinead?'

'Mmm, not very, I mean we see each other when she's over from Germany and when Beli is up from London, but not often. We're Facebook and Insta friends mostly.'

'And Neive,'

'I was closer to Mhairi.'

'So why do you think Mhairi didn't raise the alarm, call me or tell you what she'd seen?'

Kyla shook her head. 'You know the next morning, when the police were here she was acting strangely, I just thought she was in shock; then of course she disappeared and killed herself.'

'I don't think she did. I think she was silenced. She wasn't just in shock, she was terrified.'

'What? But I thought the coroner had ruled suicide, and there's finally going to be a funeral for her. Have you talked to the police about what you think?'

'I need to speak to DCI Hickson, she's been taken off the case.'

Rose noticed Kyla's face flush when she mentioned the DCI. 'What is it?'

'Hickson might be another reason why Mhairi didn't say anything about what she saw. She used to… well I'm sure it's ok to tell you. Hickson was Sinead's dad's mistress for about two years. I saw them together at a restaurant, they were being very touchy-feely, if you know what I mean. Sinead used to joke about her dad releasing the men his girlfriend arrested, or something like that. He dumped Hickson when he met Caroline, after Sinead and Amanda met her in New York.'

'Another secret! Why are you just telling me this now? And why didn't Alex say anything about that yesterday? Surely if Thornberry had dumped Hickson for Caroline, she would have been delighted to learn that her rival in love should be arrested. Hickson must have known Alex worked for Thornberry if they were that close. And Hickson told me she'd transferred here to get him for all the crimes he'd gotten away with. Mhairi not saying anything because she knew about the affair doesn't add up at all.'

179

Kyla shrugged. 'I guess none of us thought her having had a relationship with Sinead's dad was important at the time. But, if I were you I'd be careful what I told her, without someone else being there. Someone you trusted.'

'Slim pickings on who to trust, apart from my tribe that is. I don't know what I'd do without Rob, Trixie and Anthony.'

Rose plated a batch of the fresh muffins and took them over to Kyla. 'There have been way too many secrets from the beginning. But something you've just said has given me an idea. I just hope it's not leading me down another rabbit hole.'

Rose sent Anthony a text. *Any old mates who might know why Hickson transferred to Edi?* Then she called her solicitor. Her mind was racing with what she hoped was a final solution to what had really happened to Belinda, Mhairi, Amanda, and Leo.

.oOo.

'I don't know how you managed to talk me into doing this,' said Anthony, as they pulled out of the petrol station just outside Loch Leven three hours later, 'but this time it looks like you're right.'

'Did you get anywhere with your pal in London?'

'He'll contact me later, but I think he'll help.'

'So there are benefits to being a retired policeman, despite how that London lot treated you at the hospital.'

'Seems so.'

'And are there benefits to being friends with me, despite how crazy making I've been over the past few weeks?'

Anthony glanced over at her and smiled. 'Between you and Cathy it looks like I've gone from being a straight laced and uptight curmudgeon to a man I hardly recognise. My youthful self seems to have made a comeback.

'It's good,' said Rose. 'We like him,' she chuckled and leaned over to give him a peck on the cheek.

.oOo.

'Habib had more than exceeded Rose's expectations. When she and Anthony arrived in Leith for the meeting the next day, the moustached DCI, Jones, Kyla, Neive, Trixie and Rob were already assembled.

'Did you manage to put it all together?' Habib asked.

'Yep, thanks to Anthony.'

'What's all this about. As a retired policeman, I hope you know what you're risking.' The moustached DCI's thin voice spoke without authority under Habib's glare. 'This is very unorthodox.'

'My client wishes to present some information, a hypothesis about the evening Belinda Sanderson was murdered. What she has to say will need investigating. But we believe, what she has discovered, will exonerate her. She has not been found guilty and she has a right to do this, under law. At the end of this meeting she will sign an affidavit.'

The DCI looked down and sniffed. 'But anything she says can and will be...'

Habib held up her hand to stop him mid flow, 'Yes, we are aware of the risk that she could also incriminate herself. Thank you.'

'Go for it Rose,' muttered Rob.

Rose took a deep breath and looked around the room. She unrolled the piece of board she had been holding and placed it in the middle of the floor. Everyone peered down at the scrawled map of names that were connected by arrows pointing in different directions.

'I know that what I am about to say will sound implausible at first. But thanks to Anthony, I have been able to recover some CCTV footage which will, to some degree, back up what I'm going to tell you.'

'You can't be serious,' the DCI slapped his knee. 'Of all the time wasting gimmicks, this trumps anything I've heard before. Where and how did you even get CCTV footage?'

Rose glanced at Anthony.

'If you're worried that what we're about to watch was obtained under false pretences I can assure that it wasn't. And I have signed statements from the people I approached about what was said. However, whether or not it can be used in court will be up to the procurator fiscal.'

'From the beginning, as soon as DCI Hickson asked me to think about what I may or may not have heard that night, information in some form or another was missing. Information that didn't seem important to some of the gusts and friends of Belinda, including Amanda and which may have contributed to her own murder.

Kyla and Neive gasped.

'For the last almost two months I was on the verge of relapse. It hit me hard on the night of the hen party, just before I found Belinda's body. I'm not here to talk about myself, but I need to explain that because I wasn't clear headed about who I was, my relationship with Kay and perseverating and blaming myself about what had what had happened to Chris, I started chasing down all sorts of rabbit holes, imagining things about people and getting it very wrong. I believe and I think the CCTV footage will show, that the person who murdered Belinda, Amanda, Mhairi and Leo was DCI Hickson.

'Rubbish,' said the Inspector.

'Shall we watch it before passing judgement?' snapped Habib and inserted the memory stick into her laptop. 'Sorry, the one time I wish I had a smart TV,' she said as she turned the screen around. She pressed *Play*.

The first shot was of a woman in a baseball cap going into the basement of Torphichen Street. Moments later Sinead and her father arrived. The footage was dated December 22nd, the night before the hen party. 'Is that Sally?' Asked Neive.

'You'd think so wouldn't you, but that woman's just a little taller. Watch when they all come out.' The video jumped and the woman came up the stairs, she'd taken off the cap and was shouting at the man standing at the bottom of the stairs. There was no sound, but she made a fist and then pointed two fingers at him, before she walked away.'

'Oh my god, that's DCI Hickson, not Sally at all. How did she do that?'

'The same way I impersonated Sally and I'm taller too, Hickson was using a wig to change her hair. This is the following day. It's dark but there's footage of two women entering the basement. One of them is Sally, the other is DCI Hickson, again, she's dressed and wearing a wig to make herself look like Sally. Later we see Sally leaving from the front door, once the taxis have gone, and then Hickson leaving from the basement, after she murdered Belinda and attacked me.' Rose paused the footage.

'And there she is again on the 26th, wearing the same baseball cap she wore on the 22$^{nd}$, the day she had that row with Thornberry. And look who's driving the car.'

'Sally's brother, Alex!' Neive and Kyla said in unison.

'Yes, Sally and Alex were both being paid by Hickson. She'd convinced them that Angus Thornberry was after them, and that he was responsible for murdering Belinda. I couldn't understand why Alex Thornberry would be dabbling in publishing. In fact he wasn't but Hickson was. He bankrolled Sally's publications when he was with Hickson, but then he betrayed her with Caroline, the daughter of a publishing magnate. She saw a way to make it look as if Thornberry had done a deal with Belinda, under her pen name, Bea Lion. The way Belinda was posed at the pool was supposed to implicate him in the murder.'

'That's true,' piped up Jones, 'she kept trying to steer the investigation towards him in the beginning, but the guvnor wasn't buying it.'

'That's enough Jones,' said the inspector.

Rose took a breath and nodded at Jones. ' LJH Consulting is not a registered company, but it's the name Hickson uses for her business. I should have clocked the look on her face when I gave her the torn business card I found in the summerhouse.'

'But there is no CCTV on Torphichen,' said the Inspector, 'so where did this footage come from?'

'The two houses opposite and the one next door all have cameras,' said Anthony. 'We combined the footage. If Hickson had really been doing her job she would have looked into it.'

184

'Yeah, she kept insisting that the street wasn't covered. The rest of the footage shows Hickson in London on the day Leo was killed and at a petrol station in Loch Leven at the same time Mhairi was there, filling up with petrol. The only footage we don't have is the hit and run, but the reports say it was a silver Ford Focus and that's what Alex was driving when he picked her up from the house.'

'This doesn't prove anything, it's all circumstantial,' said the DCI.

'That's true, but there are inconsistencies in the case Hickson built against me. If you check dates and times you'll find Hickson wasn't at the police station or in Edinburgh the night that Leo was killed, or the following day, because she called me. She made out that Sally had been to see her at the police station, but that was a lie. Did you see Hickson taking a statement from Sally Ferguson Jones?'

Jones flushed and shook his head, then fumbled in his pocket.

'Oh, not here man, later, at the station.' The inspector scolded him like a child who'd been caught out. 'Motive?' The DCI flung his hands in the air.

'You didn't seem too worried about that when you charged me,' said Rose. 'Jealousy, revenge, a scorned woman who believed she had won the lottery when Angus Thornberry took her to bed. Then, when he dumped her for Caroline, she wanted her pound of flesh. She knew Thornberry wanted to frame Hoffman for revenge - maybe that's what gave her the idea, she pursued Hoffman to solidify her career prospects and climb the ladder. She's ambitious and completely without conscience. In many ways she's just like Hoffman. She set all sorts of red herrings in play, the signed contract for the book Sally wrote for example. The torn pages from the book that I found at Torphichen,, even the key in Belinda's luggage. Although I can't prove any of that.'

'So what about the shooting in London, why didn't she kill Caroline?'

'She's well connected is DCI Hickson. I'm sure if she'd wanted Caroline dead, she would have made sure that happened. Perhaps getting Caroline out of the country, scaring her not to come back was good enough.

'I'm still confused,' said Neive. 'How did Hickson get to the summerhouse without anyone seeing her?'

'You saw from the footage that Hickson had gone into the basement earlier, with Sally. She was dressed like Sally, so that if anyone saw her they wouldn't look twice. But when she went outside Mhairi saw two Sally's, which is what she told Leo. Leo thought she was drunk. How could there be two Sally's after all? Remember the real Sally, dressed as Belinda, stayed close to Mhairi for the rest of the evening after that, until everyone went upstairs. I'm guessing she would have come up with a credible story that stopped Mhairi from saying anything to anyone else. And, as you both,' Rose pointed to Kyla and Neive, 'were in on the plan it was only the guests from London who Mhairi needed to be sure wouldn't realise the switch.'

'Which is why we asked the taxis to come early,' said Neive.

Rose opened her hands, 'If only you had all told me what you knew and what had actually happened from the beginning, although, it was  too late for Mhairi, once she told Hickson she had seen the second woman Hickson couldn't risk Mhairi telling anyone else, or even perhaps recognising her.'

'So how did Hickson do it Rose, do you know?

'The mess I found in the summerhouse suggests Belinda put up a fight and Hickson overpowered her, She was strong, I mean she even took me down.'

'It was after you found the backpack that Hickson told me we were to investigate you.'

'Jones!'

'Sorry sir.'

'Jones is right. Hickson thought I was starting to get too close, although she was wrong about that, because I genuinely had no idea what she'd been up to until after I was arrested and talked to Kyla. I'd concluded that Caroline and Thornberry were guilty, once I realised they were lovers. I thought the shooting in London was a cover up, for what they'd done to Belinda, although I didn't see why Caroline would have her brother killed, so I had come to accept that as an accident.'

'So if ye hadnae been arrested...' pondered Trixie.

'Yeah, exactly. Hickson's been hoisted by her own petard.'

'I hope the police catch up with Sally and Alex, god - Mhairi trusted them.'

'I don't think Sally or Alex knew Hickson intended to murder Belinda. But when they realised the real reason she'd told Alex not to go and take the photographs, they were up to their necks. After Belinda was killed, they knew too much and they had to do what Hickson told them to. More secrets. When Leo talked to the police in London, it was probably one of Hickson's contacts. One of the bad ones I mean. He was so angry after Hickson had interviewed him. Then, after we found the access to the basement I think looking back on the questions she asked, Hickson was worried that Amanda might remember seeing her.'

'How did Hickson get the money to pay them, on a DCI's salary?'

Anthony responded to Rob's question. 'When Rose asked me to look into why Hickson transferred to Edinburgh I did a bit of digging. Rose said earlier that Hickson is well connected thanks to her relationship with Thornberry. She knew people who were willing to pay a lot of money for her to keep quiet. Sally was a convenient way to launder money. I doubt all the money in Sally's account was for her and Alex.'

'The same people who ratted on Hoffman in the end?'

'Some probably. The network she's created involves gangs responsible for county lines, fraud, and murder.'

The moustached DCI coughed. 'As I said before this is all conjecture. After Hoffman was arrested DCI Hickson was transferred for her own protection.'

Anthony shook his head. 'And so it goes on, or do you think turning a blind eye is going to make things better for your career? I'm glad I'm out if that's the case.'

'Do you think Sinead knew? I mean that clip of her and her Dad at the house with Hickson, it doesn't look good,' said Kyla.

'She probably knew more about her Dad than she's let on to her friends. You'll have to ask her how much she knew. And then again if you all hadn't kept so many secrets from me from the get-go.' Rose opened her hands

Neive and Kyla leaned in to each other, both of them were wet eyed as they clasped hands.

The moustached inspector stood up. 'I'm making no promises about anything, other than I will look into what's been said this afternoon.. Your client remains charged with murder.'

Habib nodded, 'Understood, we weren't expecting a miracle , but now you have different facts to pursue.'

The inspector sighed and beckoned to Jones. 'Come.' And, as he had with Hickson, Jones trotted behind his superior, obediently and without question.

# Chapter Twenty Three

Muffins on the Forth was mobbed with locals and tourists buying muffins, cakes and boxes of biscuits when Rose, Anthony and Cathy arrived. Three weeks had passed since the meeting at Habib's office.

'So?' said Rob, stepping in to give Rose a hug before she was even through the door. 'We've been on tenterhooks all morning.'

'Dropped,' said Rose. 'The DCI didn't look particularly happy, but thanks to Anthony, the CCTV footage, Caroline and Thornberry's statements the procurator fiscal agreed that any evidence the police had against me was tainted.'

'Och, ah'm, so happy. Ah couldnae hae just stood by if ye had still been on charges. Ah'd hae written to the Prime Minster!'

'OK Trixie, calm down, but if I ever need an advocate, I know who to ask. Look at this trade, it's almost four thirty and you're still busy.'

'Aye, it's a different routine here from Morrison, that was mostly morning and lunchtime traffic, this is lunchtime and afternoon.'

'It's a lovely wee shop, ah laik it very much,' said Cathy who had not been to the location before. She let go of

Anthony's arm and made her way to the counter to look at what was still left of the baking.

'Ma turn tae host tea, coffee an muffins,' said Trixie, pointing to an empty table by the window.

Rose looked at Rob and gave him a broad grin, 'She's right at home isn't she?'

Rob nodded.

'Well done Rose, you've done really well to get this up and running despite everything that's happened to you,' said Anthony, as he slid into a chair next to Cathy at the table.

'I'm lucky that I have such a great group of people who put up with me.'

Trixie brought over a tray laden with mugs of tea and a plate of assorted muffins. Cathy took one of the mugs of tea and lifted it in the air, 'Tae the members of Rose's tribe and tae Rose,' she said.

'Hear hear, said Anthony Rob and Trixie in unison. 'Tae Rose.'

'But Rose,' said Trixie, ah'm nae wantin' tae pour cold water on the celebration, for at least the rest of the year can ye please try an stay oot of any more murders!'

# Scottish words used:

| | | | | |
|---|---|---|---|---|
| Aboot | About | | Mithering | Fussing |
| Ah | I | | Movin' | Moving |
| Auld | Old | | Nae | No |
| Awright | Alright | | Naw | No |
| Aye | Yes | | Hee haw | Nothing |
| Baltic | Cold | | O' | Of |
| Braw | Good | | Och | Oh |
| Cannae | Cannot | | Oot | Out |
| Cos | Because | | Shouldnae | Shouldn't |
| Dae | Do | | Tae | To |
| Dinnae | Didn't | | Telt | Told |
| Doon | Down | | Th' morra | Tomorrow |
| Feart | Afraid | | Th' night | Tonight |
| Frae | From | | Wasnae | Wasn't |
| Guid | Good | | Wearin' | Wearing |
| Ha' | Have | | Wi' | With |
| Hame | Home | | Wid | Would |
| Havnae | Haven't | | Wis | Was |
| Heed | Head | | Whit | What |
| Intae | Into | | Willnae | Won't |
| Jist | Just | | Womin' | Women |
| Killt | Killed | | Ye | You |
| Ma' | My | | Yer | Your |
| Mak' | Make | | Yersel | Yourself |
| Mithering | Fussing | | | |

# The Cast

## Rose's Tribe:

| | |
|---|---|
| Rose McLaren | Amateur Sleuth. Owner of Muffins on Morrison |
| Rob | Rose's oldest friend |
| Trixie | Rose's apprentice |
| Anthony Chatterton | A retired policeman and friend |

## Returning Players:

| | |
|---|---|
| Olifer Hoffman alias Lance Cooper | Fraudster and Conman (First appeared in A Game of Murder) |
| DCI Hickson | Police Detective (First appeared in Murder by Stealth) |
| Dr.Kay Sandeep | Rose's friend (First appeared in Murder by Stealth) |

## For Murder in Winter:

Belinda and Amanda Sanderson (sisters)

Leo and Caroline Monkton (brother and sister)

Alex and Sally Ferguson (brother and sister)

Mhairi, Sinead, Neive and Kyla (friends)

Jones, a policeman

Habib Singh, a solicitor

Angus Thornberry, (Sinead's father)

# Rose's Banana Curry Muffins

## Ingredients:

2 cups - All Purpose Flour
2 teaspoons - Baking Powder
½ teaspoon - Baking Soda
1 ½ cups - Bran
2 ounces - Butter
1 cup - Milk or ½ cup milk and ½ cup
yoghurt combined
1 teaspoon - Curry Powder
1 tablespoon - Molasses or golden syrup
¾ cup - Banana
3 tablespoons - Condensed milk

## Method:

1. Preheat oven to 350 degrees, prepare pans.

2. Sift flour and baking powder, stir in bran and make a well in the centre.

3. Melt the butter, curry powder, treacle and condensed milk together.

4. Dissolve the soda in the milk and pour into the dry ingredients with the butter mixture and the bananas.

5. Stir until just combined.

6. Spoon into pans and bake for 15 to 20 minutes or until well risen and golden. Makes 16 to 18 muffins.

## If you enjoyed **MURDER IN MIDWINTER**

Please post a review or contact Liza via her website to let her know your comments. The books in the Rose McLaren series are:

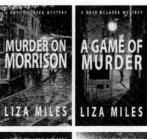

- Murder on Morrison
- A Game of Murder
- Murder By Stealth
- Murder in Midwinter

You can keep in touch with Liza and find out about advance notice about her other work in progress. Sign up to a quarterly newsletter or connect via social media:

Facebook and Instagram: www.lizamileswriter.com
Newsletter – www.linktr.ee/lizamileswriter

Liza's work is available on Amazon, can be requested in libraries and from local bookshops or via her website:

- Love Bites – a book of short stories about the ups and downs of relationships
- My Life's Not Funny – a standalone coming-of-age novel
- An ABC of Thanks – an early reading resource for young children, caregivers and parents. (Published as Mary-Beth Mazzini) by Mad Cat Publishing